Little Ann

Growing Up

J. P. Leonard
2/5/2019

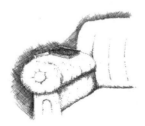

Ann deals with the problems and challenges of life while doing her best to learn how to grow up.

Contents

Chapter 1

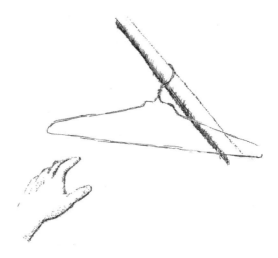

This is a story about a little girl named Ann. She wasn't just little in age; she was also little in stature. She was so small that she couldn't reach the hangers in the clothes closet in her bedroom. Instead, she had to fold her clothes and place them in boxes on the floor near her bed.

The problem with doing that was Duster and Buster, the family cat and dog. Their original names were Michelle and Mike, but because their large, fluffy tails would either gather great dust bunnies or knock things off tables and chairs, Ann renamed them Duster and Buster. She didn't mind that their fluffy tails collected dust and broke things; but the two of them insisted on using the boxes that were packed with her clothes for their beds at night. The troublesome part of this was that they made all her clothes smell just as bad as Duster and Buster did.

Not only was Ann short in stature she also had frizzy hair that only did what it wanted, which was always something bad. Ann was at the age when she was losing her baby teeth. Her two front teeth were missing, which made her speak with a lisp and spray spit when she tried to talk. As a result, the other children at school didn't want to talk with her and wouldn't sit near her at lunch time. Her teacher moved her from a desk at the front of the classroom to one in the back of the room to avoid the spray and wouldn't call on her even if Ann waved her hand and arm wildly.

In addition to her being short, spitting when she lisped, and smelling like a dog and cat, Ann had a problem with her name. Her last name was Dee. The other kids teased her mercilessly, calling her Andy. It was more than a person could stand! She even asked her mother why she had been named Ann.

Her mother was a tall, slim young woman with fine features and a melodic voice; everything that Ann wished *she* could be. Her mother listened intently to Ann's question about her name and then explained with a soft smile that her own name was Ann and that she and her father, Andy,

were so happy to have a little girl that they wanted to give

her her mother's name. Little Ann just rolled her eyes and

said that was probably fine when her mother's last name

was Harrison, but now the other children just called her

Andy. What was even worse was that her father's middle

name was Douglas so that he was Andy D. Dee, which made

it sound like he was stuttering when he used his formal

name. Her mother just smiled a very kind smile and told Ann

that she loved her. All Ann could do was roll her eyes again.

Ann loved math more than any other subject except

maybe music. She found every book her parents had in their

house on math and read about geometry. Neither of those

subjects was taught in her math class, but she always hoped

that the teacher just might finally call on her. She would then have a chance to explain how an isosceles triangle had two equal sides and how music and math were related in an almost magical way. So far her arm waving never inspired her teacher, Mrs. Crisp, to call on her.

Recess and lunch were tough times for Ann because the other girls didn't ask her to join in with the recess activities and nobody wanted to sit with her when they had lunch in the cafeteria. So during recess she would sit outside alone on the concrete walkway and play jacks by herself. She got pretty good at the game, but her hands were so small that she never could fit all ten jacks and the ball in her fist. That was okay since her set of jacks was missing two of them so she could only go up to eight jacks anyway.

The best part of the school day for Ann was getting on the bus and heading for home. Because no one wanted to sit next to her, she would be by herself looking out the window thinking about music and geometry. The other kids used to throw things at her or taunt her by calling her Andy. Thankfully, over time, they had grown bored and now left her alone to stare out the window of the bus.

When the yellow bus finally reached her street she could see Duster sitting in an open upstairs window with her yellow fur pressed up against the wire of the window screen. As the brakes squealed the bus to a stop, Buster appeared out of nowhere. His enthusiasm was only outdone by the size of his wagging tail. It was as if some trickster had taken a tail from a much larger dog and grafted it onto his skinny body. His whole body wagged along with his tail as he waited for Ann to step off the bus. Ann gave a big sigh as the kids would sarcastically ask what kind of animal Duster was. They would ask if he was an alien or some kind of science experiment. Ann just ignored their taunts and patted Buster on the head as they walked to the front steps and she repositioned the few books she had in her arms. Buster's grey fur was full of snarls and twigs and burrs that it had gathered during his day of wandering about the yard and sleeping on the roots of a large tree in the back corner of the lot.

Ann had once tried to brush out his matted coat and became exhausted after just a few minutes of trying. Her efforts just seemed to make it worse. The wire brush she had used was soon clogged with goodness knows what and his fur looked just about the same as when she had started.

Duster, on the other hand, would groom herself for hours spending extra time on her tail. When she was done, the fur on her tail was all lined up and licked so that it started out looking like a thin cat's tail. However, after she found a sunny spot to stretch out in, the hairs would dry and her tail became a large duster again.

Ann went inside the house with Buster trailing after her. She stopped in the kitchen and found her mother humming a pleasant melody as she worked on the ingredients to make an apple pie. Her mother had washed some apples and was busy cutting them up. She carefully sliced off the peels and then cut the bare apples into pieces, removing the cores as she went. There was a wonderful smell as her mother put together brown sugar and cinnamon with butter. She would eventually mix them in with the apples that were going to be filling the pie shell.

"Do you want to help, Ann?" she asked.

Ann shook her head, climbed up on the tall kitchen stool, and then rested her elbows on the counter as she watched the process. She loved to watch her mother cook and delighted in the final outcome, but she really didn't enjoy struggling with the preparations. She was just too small compared to all the big stirring spoons and bowls. She always seemed to make a mess no matter how careful she tried to be, ending up being very frustrated and disappointed.

Her mother went back to humming her melody and wearing a sweet smile on her face as she worked the ingredients, waiting for the oven to warm enough for baking.

When Ann saw that the pie making was complete and ready to be popped into the oven she carefully climbed down from the stool and headed up to her room, grabbing her school books and bag of jacks as she went.

"Supper will be ready when your father gets home around six," her mother called after her as Ann headed for the stairs.

It was always the same. It was a Friday so Ann expected her father to be home later than six. He often had a project to get done before the weekend and that meant a long work day for him on Fridays. That extra time at work on

Friday would mean that he had all Saturday to spend at home instead of going back to work for a half day.

Ann climbed the stairs and stopped at the landing that was formed so the stairs could turn with the corner of the wall. At the landing there was a bookshelf built into the wall which held their family library. Ann could only reach books that were on a couple of the bottom shelves. She had to find a chair or step ladder if she wanted to get to more of the books on the higher shelves. She found that she could stand on the higher stairs and at least see the titles on the spines of the books up high. Thankfully, the bottom shelves contained the math and music books that she found so fascinating. She looked over the titles, recognizing the ones that she had already spent time reading. She was hoping that there might be some book squeezed between the volumes that she had missed. Nope, they were all the ones that she knew about.

With a big sigh and a small spray from the gap from her missing front teeth she plucked out the geometry book that was on the bottom shelf. Even though she had read through it once, she found it a very likeable book and thought it would be fun to reread. So she grabbed it and brought it to her room. She put her school books on the floor next to the boxes where she kept her clothes. Her bag of jacks went on top of the school books so that she would remember to take them with her on Monday morning. Her bed was just a mattress on top of a box spring on the floor and pushed up against the wall. Although she had made her bed before she left for school, Ann could tell that her mother

had come in and fixed a few flaws in her bed-making. The

sheet was tucked in at the foot of the bed and covered with

a smoothed-out comforter. Ann sighed. Not with

frustration, but with a mix of feelings. One of the feelings

came from knowing that her mother cared enough to make

her poor room look as nice as possible. The other feeling was

that she might just be a disappointment to her mother by

not being as tidy as she should when she made up her bed in

the morning.

Ann sat on her bed and opened the text on geometry,

flipping to the section on triangles, her current favorite

chapter. There was the equilateral, which she thought was

boring, the isosceles, and the scalene which was the wild

one. Nothing on it was the same. Not the angles, not the dimensions of the sides. There was the right triangle, the acute, and the obtuse which was also a scalene. She stared at the illustrations and imagined how each one would be if they were actual objects. Triangles were so stable no matter what kind they were. If you made a square out of Popsicle sticks with fasteners at each corner you could move the sides so that it was a parallelogram. If you did the same with a triangle it would just stay the same.

She hadn't spent much time with the later sections of the book because of her fascination with the properties of the triangles. This afternoon she decided to look further.

There was the pentagon with five sides, the hexagon with six. Then an octagon with eight, and it went on. A nonagon! Who would have thought? Then there was the

dodecagon. These were becoming circles! She thought of

how circles were maybe a bunch of angles with so many

small sides that they blended into a smooth shape. How

could she find out, she wondered?

Just then she heard her mother calling her down for

supper. She had been so absorbed in her thoughts that she

hadn't even heard her father come home. She jumped up

and fell over Buster as she headed downstairs. He squealed

with surprise, then just slapped his tail against the floor as if

he understood that she hadn't meant to trip over him.

"Sorry, Buster," she said and headed down the stairs

to the kitchen where the small table was that had been set

for dinner.

Her father was there sitting at the table looking

hungry, and tired. Her mother took a bowl of warm rolls

wrapped in a kitchen towel and placed them on the table.

The table was just big enough for the three of them and

their plates; still she was able to squeeze in the small bowl of

rolls. On the plates she had already dished out their meal. It

consisted of some meatloaf, potatoes, and some fresh green

beans. It was almost seven o'clock and Ann realized that she

was very hungry. She could handle the meatloaf and

mashed potatoes. She had to maneuver the green beans

around to her side teeth so that she could bite and chew

them.

While Ann concentrated on eating, her parents talked

between themselves about the weekend to come. In the

back of her brain she thought she heard her name being mentioned.

"What do you think of that, Ann?" said her mother.

Ann looked up with a cheek full of masticated green beans and tried to answer without blowing them out back on to her plate.

"Wff?," was all that came out, except for some pieces of green beans.

"Your father has a little trip for you to take with him tomorrow. He needs to inspect a bridge that his company is constructing and would like to take you along."

That had given Ann time to clear her mouth enough to speak. "What would I do?" Ann asked.

"You and your father would drive out to the construction site and he would show you around while he inspects things."

Ann thought about this. Usually her father had projects to do around their house. He worked on fixing plumbing or mowed the lawn, or sometimes helped with cleaning windows. This would be very different. Usually if there was a trip in the car they would all go together, and she would sit in the back and try not to get car sick. This trip might be interesting. Maybe she could sit in the front seat!

"Dad, how early will we have to get up?" she asked.

"We can take our time and have breakfast, Ann. As long as I can get there an hour or so before noon, that should be good enough," Andy said.

Ann liked the idea so much she started to smile and then, self-conscious about the gap in her teeth, she limited it to a lip smile. She had finished her mashed potatoes and most of the meatloaf, leaving the rest of the green beans for her to get through. She focused hard on that task until she finally had the last fork full in her mouth.

"Who would like some apple pie?" asked her mother.

Andy and Ann raised their hands and smiled. The scent of the freshly baked apple pie had filled the house all afternoon.

Ann's mother put pie slices on small plates, setting them in front of everyone's place at the table. There was hardly a crumb left on the little plates five minutes later.

Andy got up from the table and gave his wife a kiss. "That was a wonderful supper, Dear. I think I'll go in the living room and read today's paper."

"Would you help me with the dishes, Ann?" she asked.

"Okay, Mom," Ann replied and went over to the tall kitchen stool and slid it over by the sink. Her mother washed and rinsed the dishes and flatware then handed them over to Ann to dry and stack in the dish rack. When they were done and put away, Ann slid off the stool and pushed it back in its place.

"Thank you, Dear, and what will you do now?"

"I'm going to read, Mom."

"Still enjoying the books on geometry, then?"

"Yes, I'm reading about a dodecagon."

"Be sure to save time for a bath tonight, Ann."

"Okay, Mom."

Ann climbed the stairs to her room and the geometry book. Her window was open and the screen was letting in a nice breeze. The temperature had cooled down as evening approached. Duster was stretched out in her window and Buster was curled up in one of her clothes boxes.

Ann decided to take the book down to the back yard while it was still light out. There was an old wooden bench near the large tree with the huge roots that protruded from the ground and made it look like the tree was trying to lift them out of the ground and walk to another part of the yard.

Ann often sat on the big roots, but this time she placed the book open on the nearby bench and lay down on her elbows to read the text.

The minutes passed and the light dimmed to twilight on its way to darkness. Ann decided that it was time to head back into the house. She went past her father, who had fallen asleep on the couch in the front room while he was reading the newspaper. Ann put the book back in its place on the shelf as she climbed upstairs. She went to peek in the bathroom and her mother was there ready to fill the tub.

"Hi honey, I saw that you were coming in so I thought I would get your bath ready."

Ann went to the bathroom closet and pulled out a towel and washcloth as the warm water filled the tub. While she waited for the tub to fill Ann brushed her teeth. Her mother hummed a little tune and in a couple of minutes the bath was ready for Ann. She stepped out of her clothes and climbed over the edge of the tub into the warm water.

"Let me know when you are done Dear," said her Mom, and closed the bathroom door.

Ann spent time getting cleaned and then just lay back in the water thinking about her day and what she had seen in the geometry book. She wondered about how she could turn triangles into circles. She wanted to find the chapter on circles and see if it could tell her.

"Ann, are you still in there?" came a voice from the other side of the door. It was her mother.

"I'm just getting out now, Mom," she answered.

Ann had almost drifted off to sleep. Her finger tips had gotten all wrinkly from being in the water so long.

She flipped the drain to let the water flow out as she dried off. Then she wrapped the towel around herself. She hung the washcloth over the edge of the tub and headed across the hall to her room.

On the bed were some night clothes that her mother had laid out for her. That brought her a smile as she changed into them before she went back in the bathroom to hang the towel over the rack in there.

Back in her room she closed her window, shooing Duster onto the bedroom floor. She climbed under the covers and stared out of her window, watching the tree

branches sway in the evening breeze. Tomorrow promised

to be an adventure.

Chapter 2

Ann awoke as the sunlight bounced off the windows of the building across the street and filtered through the branches of the trees out by the sidewalk. She didn't have a clock in her room, but she could hear her parents downstairs preparing for the day. She quickly changed into her clothes and descended the stairs on her way to the kitchen. Her mother turned to smile at her as she entered the room.

"Good morning, Ann."

"'Morning, Mom," she replied. "Where's Dad?"

"He is outside working on the car. He was going to get some gas for it, but it won't start."

"Oh, no!" Ann thought that the planned adventure might not happen.

"Don't worry, Ann; your Dad is good at fixing things, and I haven't quite made breakfast yet."

"What's for breakfast?" she lisped.

"We are running short on eggs, but I can make pancakes with blueberries. How would you like that?"

Ann just loved pancakes, especially with blueberries, so without thinking she smiled a huge smile that featured the big gap in her front teeth.

"I don't have any syrup, but I can make some whipped cream," said her mother with a smile. Ann's mouth was watering with the thought and she grinned even wider.

Her mother pulled out a large mixing bowl from the cabinet and started mixing the pancake batter. With the crack of an egg and the addition of some milk and mix all she had to do was stir it up. Next, she took out a smaller bowl and poured in some heavy cream that she whipped into a lovely froth. She was about to spoon some blueberries into the pancake mix when her husband came in with a strong smell of gasoline on him.

"How is it coming, Dear?" she asked.

"It's not fixed yet, Honey. It looks like the fuel filter is clogged."

"How do we fix that?"

"Well, I'll have to get over to an auto parts store. There is one a couple of miles away from us. I can buy a new filter there, bring it home, and install it."

"Good gracious, how will you get to the parts store then?"

"I could walk. That would take quite a while. I think I remember an old bicycle down in the basement that might still work. That would save me a lot of time."

"Well, breakfast will be ready in just about five minutes, so wash up and have something to eat first, Dear."

"Will do, honey." He disappeared into the downstairs bathroom to clean up while pancake batter sizzled on the pan. In a few minutes he was back to see that the stack was being piled high with just a couple more to be made.

"Anything that I can do to help?" he asked.

"Sure, the whipped cream is ready so you can put the bowl on the table and sit down."

As he sat down he turned to Ann and asked, "How are you this morning, Princess?"

"I'm fine Dad." Ann did feel fine, even though she was also a little worried that the car might take a long time to fix, and that would jeopardize the chance for her to go to the work site with her father.

Plates with blueberry pancakes arrived at the table, just as her mother had promised.

After breakfast Ann helped her mother clean up the dishes while her father explored the basement looking for the bicycle. There were a lot of sounds coming from the cellar as Andy searched and moved old junk from one pile to another.

Soon Ann and her mother had the dishes done and the kitchen straightened up. It was pleasant enough for the kitchen window to be open. The screen door also let in a nice breeze.

Her father came up from below with what looked like a wreck of a bicycle in his arms. He hauled it to the back porch and Ann held the screen door open for him. Once the bicycle was outside in the sun, it was clear that while it had once been a reliable mode of transportation it needed a lot of help now. The chain was hanging loosely off the gears,

both tires were flat and there were no replacements. From

Ann's point of view it looked hopeless.

Her Dad took a rag out of his pocket and swatted

away the dust and cobwebs. Attached to the back of the

seat was a small leather bag. Andy unbuckled the two straps

and fished around inside the bag.

"Aha!" he exclaimed. His fingers came out with a

bunch of things Ann had never seen before. There was a

small container, some metal pieces, and more stuff.

"What is all that?" Ann wondered.

"It is a kit to fix flat bicycle tires. I just hope that the

patches are still good."

Ann sat down, crossed her legs, put her elbows on her knees. She wasn't sure what he was talking about, but it was certainly interesting.

Her father laid out the contents that he had pulled out of the small bag and then opened the small can with a metal top.

"Ah good!" he exclaimed. He dumped out the container and out fell some square, flat, black pieces and a small tube. A smile came across his face and he turned to Ann and winked.

"I'll be right back, Princess." he said, and disappeared for a minute or two.

When he returned he had his bag of wrenches with him. He pulled out two wrenches and loosened the nuts holding the wheel to the front fork of the bicycle. With the wheel released he used two metal spoon-like objects to pry the tire off the metal rim. Inside of the tire was a large round tube, what he called the "inner tube". He looked over the tube very carefully, squinting hard.

"What do you see Daddy?" asked Ann.

"Nothing, and that's good."

"Will the tire work again?"

"I think so, but first I've got to blow it up and check for leaks in order to be certain."

"How can you do that?"

"Just watch," he said with a smile. His hands went back to the bicycle and he took hold of part of the frame and pulled it off.

"Oh, no!" said Ann, "You broke it!"

Andy laughed and said, "It's okay, Princess. This is supposed to detach. It's a tire pump."

He pulled out a small hose that was hidden inside the black tube. He screwed the hose into one end and then pulled both ends apart. It became longer, and had a smaller silver rod connecting both ends. He then pushed it back together, creating a small whooshing sound. He attached the hose to the big round black inner tube and worked the tire pump in and out, causing the big black inner tube to inflate. The inner tube got larger and looked like a tire, sort of.

"Ann, go get me a spray bottle of cleaner, would you?"

Ann got up and went into the kitchen and looked in the cabinet under the sink and found what her father had asked for. She brought it back to him and he sprayed it all over the inner tube.

"Is it that dirty?"

Andy smiled again. "No Princess, this will tell me if it leaks."

"How?"

"Now that I've put air under pressure in the inner tube, if it leaks it will blow out air and the spray cleaner will make bubbles where air is leaking out."

Ann looked carefully at the black inner tube and saw there were no bubbles at all. Her father declared that it was fine and put it back on the wheel. Then he used the metal tools to pry the tire onto the wheel rim. When it was all back together Andy pumped up the inner tube using the black part that poked out of the wheel and into the area where the metal spokes were. The tire got nice and round.

Andy put the wheel back on the bicycle's front forks and then removed the rear wheel. He took the tire off the rear rim and did the same test of the inner tube. This time there were bubbles in one spot.

"Uh oh," said Ann.

"Yep, a leak," said Andy, "but all is not lost. I think this patch kit will still work."

He handed the inner tube to Ann and told her to pinch her fingers together right where the bubbles had come out while he got the parts to the patch kit. Ann pinched hard and waited while her father got the patch, the can that had held the patches, and the small tube that had been inside of the can.

Andy carefully took the inner tube from Ann and placed it so that the part that had produced bubbles was face up and was flattened out. Then he took the metal top of the can and Ann saw for the first time that it had a bunch of holes in it almost like a cheese grater. Andy rubbed these against the area of the inner tube where he was going to fix

the leak. From the repair kit he opened the tube that looked

like a tiny tube of toothpaste and squeezed out a clear gel

onto the spot he had rubbed. Then he took one of the black

squares, peeled off a thin red piece off of it and pressed the

patch on the area of the leak. He rubbed the patch hard and

often as he squeezed it onto the inner tube.

"What is that going to do, Dad?"

"It will glue itself to the inner tube, sealing the hole."

"What were you doing with the cheese grater?"

Andy laughed, "That was to rough up the surface of

the tube so that the patch would glue more tightly to it.

There, I think it's all set."

He put the tube and tire back together, pumped up the tire, and put the wheel back on the bicycle frame being careful to set the chain properly on the gears. When he had completed that, he smiled with satisfaction and patted the bicycle on its seat.

"OK, tell your mother I've gone to the parts store and will be back soon, Princess." Her father carried the bicycle down the back steps and around to the front of the house where he jumped on the bike and headed into town.

As Ann watched her father ride away, her attention was caught by the spinning spokes of the bicycle's wheels. There again were a bunch of long, skinny triangles where the triangles defined a circle. She pondered this, and walked back inside the house.

"Mom, Daddy got the bicycle fixed and he is going to get a part for our car," She told her mother.

"What will you do while you wait?" her mother asked.

"I don't know."

"Why don't we see what we can do differently with your hair?'

Ann groaned. Running a brush or comb through her hair was probably the most excruciating thing in the world she could think of.

"Don't worry, Ann, I'll take it slow and easy. I have an idea that we can try. I think you will like it."

"Okay, Mom," Ann sighed, "I trust you." She really didn't. She remembered the last time they had tried this she felt as if her scalp was being torn from her head and she cried real tears of agony.

"Good, I have a special hair brush that a friend recommended. I need to get it from my room. Why don't you get your teeth brushed and meet me on the porch off the back of the kitchen. Can you handle getting the stool on the porch?"

"I think so."

Her mother headed up the stairs and Ann followed her, stopping at the bathroom to brush her teeth. Back down the stairs she went into the kitchen to get the stool that she often sat on while she watched her mother cook. She grabbed the stool by two of its legs and lifted it a couple of inches off the floor. It was too heavy for her to carry so she tipped it over and resorted to dragging it to the back door. Then she opened the screen door and propped it open with a box that was on the porch. Grabbing the seat of the stool she leaned it over so she could drag its legs over the threshold and onto the porch's wooden planked floor. It took a lot of effort. She stood the stool back on its legs and then removed the box from the propped open screen door.

Ann wondered if she should stay on the porch and endure the agony of having her hair brushed or else go out in the back yard and try to climb the old tree and hide there until her father returned. Too late! Her mother appeared at the screen door with a smile and a strange looking hair brush. At least Ann assumed it was a hair brush. It was like a brush with a handle but instead of lots of bristles it had a few long, large diameter bristles with little balls on the end.

"Scoot yourself onto the stool and I'll see what we can do to untangle your hair, Sweetheart."

Ann climbed and pulled herself up onto the seat of the stool. She crossed her legs, clenched her eyes shut tightly, and interlaced her fingers in a tight grip in her lap while she waited for the pain to start.

He mother went around to Ann's back and started by gathering up some hair in one hand while she worked with the brush in her other hand. With short strokes her mother pulled the brush through Ann's rat's nest of hair a little at a time.

Ann was surprised. Sure there was some pulling, but

it was nowhere near as painful as the last time. It actually

felt good as her mother worked her way down from the back

of Ann's head with the brush. Ann started to relax a bit.

"How does that feel, Ann?"

"OK, I think."

"Well, it is looking pretty good, Dear."

Ann felt her mother moving to the top and then sides

of her head and still the process was not as painful as it had

been the other times they had tried this. It was hardly

painful at all, just once in a while when her mother came to

a particularly tangled patch of hair and even that wasn't bad.

As her mother cleared most of the tangles, she ran the brush through all of Ann's hair. It was amazing that it actually felt good and didn't make Ann cry at all.

"There, done," her mother declared.

"Really?" Ann couldn't believe it.

"Yes, Dear, go upstairs and take a look in the mirror."

Ann was amazed. Not only was the process over, but her hair also looked different now that it was all brushed out. She came out of the bathroom with a huge smile on her face despite missing two of her front teeth.

"Oh, Mom, it's wonderful!"

"Let's try one more thing," said her mother, as she disappeared into her bedroom.

In a Moment her mother appeared with a piece of ribbon in her hand and turned Ann around while she looped it from the back of her neck to the top of her head and tied a bow.

"Look at it now, Ann."

Ann could not believe her eyes. She really did feel like a Princess.

Chapter 3

"Hello, Princess!" It was her father. He had returned from his errand at the auto parts store. In his hand was a small box that Ann presumed was the fuel filter that their car needed.

"My goodness, Ann, you look lovely,'" he exclaimed.

Ann blushed and smiled.

"Andy, did you get the part you needed?" her mother asked.

"Yes, and I had a bit of an adventure getting it. I rode down to the parts store on the bicycle that I rescued from the cellar and left it outside while I went in the store to get the correct part. When I came out the bicycle was gone!"

"Oh my, how did you manage to get back home so quickly?" asked his wife.

"One of our neighbors was driving by as I was walking back and gave me a ride. I couldn't believe my luck. It would have taken another half hour for me to have walked all the way back."

"Will you still be able to fix the car, Daddy?" asked Ann.

"I think so. I am going back outside and crawl under the car to do just that. I was going to ask you to come out and help me, but your hair looks so nice that you'd better not. I'm likely to get all dirty and smelly replacing the fuel filter. You can still watch me if you want."

Ann thought that would be fine and followed him outside to the front yard and sat down on the front steps where she had a pretty good vantage point. Her father got out a large piece of cardboard and used it to slide on so he could get under the back of the car. He had previously detached the old fuel filter from the rubber fuel lines and had an old pan to let some of the fuel drip in while things were disconnected. He had to disconnect them again because he had put the old filter back on the lines to stop the fuel flow while he went and got the new filter. He got up from under the car to find something to clamp the hoses to keep them from pouring out fuel. It was getting warmer outside and the breeze had picked up as the morning wore on.

"Come on, Princess, and let's see if there is anything down in the cellar that I can use to clamp off the fuel lines."

He and Ann headed down the creaky stairs to the cellar once again. As her father poked around the jars and shelves for something appropriate to clamp the fuel lines, Ann did her own exploring. There were only a couple of bare light bulbs to illuminate the cellar. The longer they were down there the more that their eyes adjusted and the brighter it seemed to get.

"Aha!" her father remarked.

He had been poking around in an old metal tool box and came across some things that looked like pairs of scissors without any cutting blades.

"What are those?" she asked.

"These are some clamps that doctors or surgeons use. They are called Kelly clamps. They will work for what I need."

"How?"

"Watch - as I tighten them they automatically lock tight." He squeezed the ring ends together with a clicking sound. Sure enough, they were locked together.

"Then I can unlock them with another squeeze as I pull them apart." He gave them a little squeeze and then moved the ring ends apart.

Her father smiled a smile of satisfaction and he said, "Let's go back to the car and get this new filter installed!"

They went out to the car and her father slid back underneath with the cardboard sheet under his back. She could hear the Kelly clamps clicking and her father working on installing the new filter. In a Moment he was out from under the car and pulling out the cardboard sheet and the old steel pan that he had used to catch any dripping fuel. In the pan was the old fuel filter.

"Here, look at this," he said as he took the old filter and turned it so one of its tubes faced the old steel pan. Hardly anything came out so he then turned it so the other end faced the pan and some fuel and clumps of rust dripped out into the pan.

"See how clogged it was?"

"Hmm, will the new one fix it?"

"It should. The old filter trapped all the junk that was coming out of the fuel tank before it could get into the engine and really mess things up, so when the junk piled up, it wouldn't let enough fuel through to feed the engine."

"How did the junk get in the fuel tank?" asked Ann.

"There are several reasons. Over time the fuel tank, which is made of metal, rusted some. Sometimes the filling stations run low on gasoline in their storage tanks and so any dirt in their tanks is pumped from the bottom of it into our car's fuel tank."

"Well – will this fix our car?"

"I'm going to put fresh fuel in the car's tank, so there should be a lot more clean fuel in there than any dirt that might be left. The new filter will take care of that."

"Hmm," said Ann as she thought about what he had said.

"Let your mother know that I'm off to get the car's tank filled and I'll be back shortly."

"Alright, Dad."

Her father got into the car to start it. At first, only the sound of the starter turning was all she could hear. After a bit of time the engine fired up and her father pulled out of the driveway.

Ann looked at the pan with the old filter and gasoline in it. The Kelly clamps were on the ground beside it and she went over and picked one up to try herself. They clicked a couple of times as she squeezed it, then it became hard to squeeze it more. When she tried to pull it apart it was stuck solid. After some experimentation she found that if she put as much pressure as she could muster squeezing it and then moving the grips away from each other, the clamp would come loose and she could click them shut again. It was a lot harder than when her father did it with one hand.

She went back to the front steps and continued to work the Kelly clamp, listening to the clicks and squeezing it to get it loose again. She was concentrating so much that she almost didn't notice the sound of gravel as her father drove the car up the driveway.

"We're almost ready to take our road trip to the construction site, Ann. Just let me get cleaned up a bit."

He gathered up the clamps, pan, cardboard, and other tools that he had used. He poured the small amount of gasoline from the pan into a container that he kept used oil in. Then he wiped out the pan with an old rag that he tossed into their outside trash barrel and went down in the cellar and put the tools away. When he went upstairs to wash up, Ann went into the kitchen to see where her mother was. She saw that she wasn't in the kitchen. Instead she was on the back porch preparing some carrots to be cooked.

"Hi Mom," Ann said as she opened the screen door to the porch.

"How is your father coming with the car?"

"He changed the filter and then went and got the gas tank filled up. He's getting cleaned up."

"Wonderful, so I expect you two will be heading off soon."

"Yes."

"Why don't you pick out a couple of apples from the table, in case you and your Dad get hungry?"

"OK." Ann went back through the screen door and into the kitchen where the fruit bowl was. She picked out two apples, one yellow and the other a deep red. She found a small paper bag, put the two apples in it, and headed to

the front of the house. Her father had cleaned up and was

just coming to the bottom of the stairs.

"Ready to go, Princess?"

"Ready, Dad."

"Let me say goodbye to your mother; you go ahead

out to the car, OK?"

"Okay."

Ann headed out through the front door to the car.

She opened the front passenger door and stopped. She

could get herself in the front seat. Ann could tell that she

wouldn't be able to see over the dashboard. Ann groaned,

thinking of how much she had been looking forward to being

in the front seat for a change as she couldn't see much out of the car when she was stuck in the back seat.

She closed the front door and opened the back one and stared at the booster seat that she rode in when she sat in the car.

"Hold on, Princess and I will move that to the front for you!"

It was her father, and he reached in to undo the latches that held in the booster seat. In just a few seconds it was in the front passenger seat and he was securing it in place.

"Now you can use the seat belt."

Ann climbed aboard the seat and waited while her father pulled the belt around her and clicked it securely to the latch. She could see a little better than she had ever been able to from the back seat. The dashboard was not in her way like the headrests were when she was in the back seat. It was still a little tough for her to see over it.

"Hold on one second there, Ann..."

Her father brought the seat forward just a bit and up higher. Now Ann could really see and a smile spread across her face.

"There you go, Princess," said her father and he walked around to sit in the driver's seat.

He backed the car out, put it in drive, and they were off on their adventure.

Ann was quiet as they drove along the streets of the town. She was busy just looking at everything. When she rode the school bus she never saw that much and was busy trying to ignore the other children and be as inconspicuous as possible. That usually meant just looking out the bus window or at the floor.

On this ride she had a wonderful view and her eyes were busy taking it all in. There were buildings and stores and houses. There were streets that she had never been down before. Soon there were more trees than houses. Her father then took a turn that brought them to a highway and much more traffic. She was amazed at all the cars and trucks that filled the road. There were many more lanes too.

Cars and trucks passed them on both sides and she

wondered how her father knew where to go.

"How do you know where you are going?" she asked.

"Oh, I've been out to this construction site a few times

now. Early on I had to work with the surveyors so I could get

the information I needed to work with the engineers that

designed the bridge."

"What are surveyors?"

"They are people who know how to use instruments

to measure the land and determine the boundaries of

things. It is very important work because engineers need to

understand the contours of the land that they design their

projects for. They also need to know the exact length that their designs must be. You wouldn't want a bridge that was too short or one that wasn't level with the road. The surveyors take measurements at the site where construction will take place, and the engineers then have the information they need to design a bridge that will match the topography."

"What do you mean 'topography'?"

"I mean the actual shape of the land. It may not look it, but the ground isn't perfectly flat. It has ups and downs we call contours. The land itself is made up of all different soils like clay, rocks, and sand. There are people called geologists who take samples of the soil and rocks so that the design engineers know where to build the supporting structures. A bridge can't be built on soft areas. The weight of the bridge would cause it to sink and fall down."

Ann was quiet as she thought about what her father had explained. She wasn't sure that she really understood it all, though parts of it made sense.

"It won't be much longer and we will be at the site," Andy said, "and I can show you what I am talking about."

Soon they came to an area of the highway where there were all kinds of orange signs and orange cones. Her father stopped the car and told her to stay put while he opened a gate. Then they drove onto a dirt road to the bridge.

Ann climbed out of the car, looked around and could see a bridge that spanned a small river. The road they drove in on was dirt, and here and there were piles of more dirt and gravel, along with pieces of steel that she could not identify. As she stared at the bridge she saw something familiar. It was a metal bridge with lots of angled bits of steel. What she recognized were all the triangles that were formed by the metal pieces and held together by the rivets.

"Dad, look at the triangles!"

"What? Oh yes, I see what you mean. The triangles are made of steel and ensure that the bridge's structure is rigid where it needs to be. This is an older bridge and needs to be rehabilitated because of the amount of traffic that will now be using it. We are adding metal gussets to where the corners of the triangles meet. That will make the bridge a lot stronger and allow it to continue to be used for many more years. Otherwise it would have to be torn down and a whole new one would have to be built."

"What are gussets?"

"Here are some on the ground that haven't been put into place yet."

They were large pieces of flat steel with holes in them. The steel was quite thick and Ann wondered how heavy they were.

"These will be put into the corners of the triangles and new rivets will be installed so that the triangles will be stronger than they are now. You can see that a few have

been put in place on the far end of the bridge"

Just then a truck came down the dirt road they had

just traveled on. It was kicking up a lot of dust and the driver

pulled it up close to them and stopped in a cloud of dust and

dirt.

Chapter 4

A tall, thin man just about leaped from the driver's door with a grim look. In an instant his eyes lost their stern look and a smile appeared on his face.

"Well, Andy! I saw the gate open and unlocked and I thought it might be someone trying to steal some of the material we have stored on the construction site. I'm sure glad it was just you," he said through his grin.

"Bruce, I'd like you to meet my daughter, Ann. - Ann, this is Mr. Jenkins."

Ann wasn't quite sure what to make of this big fellow. He put out his hand so she gave him hers and said, "Hello, Mr. Jenkins."

"Please, call me Bruce, and nice to meet you, Ann." He said as he shook her hand.

His hand was large and powerful; even so he was gentle as he shook her hand. She could feel kindness in the grip and she could tell that these were working hands with skin that was worn and tough.

"I was showing Ann the project that we are working on and explaining what changes are being made to the bridge to allow it to handle more traffic."

"Your Dad is a mighty smart man, Ann. He is the engineer that found a way to keep this old bridge in place. Without his changes we would have had to tear the whole thing down and put up a new one, and that would have been very expensive."

Ann suppressed a smile because she didn't want to show her missing teeth, but her mouth curled up at the corners anyway. She felt proud of her father. She hadn't really known what he did for work until today.

"Bruce, would you show her the metal gussets? I need to take some of the rivets we are using to make certain that they are of the correct metallurgy. There have been

reports of problems with installing them."

"Sure thing, Andy. Ann, let's take a look at these big

metal things over here." Mr. Jenkins and Ann walked over to

the piles of metal while Andy headed for a storage bin. The

metal pieces were thick and had an odd triangular shape

that was rounded where the corners of a triangle would be.

They also had large holes at each of the round corners.

"These are very heavy, Ann. We can't pick them up by

hand they are so heavy. Here, see if you can lift one."

Ann put her little hands under the edge of one of the

gussets and gave it a try. It was like trying to pick up a

house. Then Bruce gave it a try and lifted the metal plate a fraction of an inch before he had to drop it. It made a muffled clang as it dropped back on the stack.

"These will be installed at the places where the bridge struts need reinforcement. First the old rivets will be cut out, and then, with the help of a machine to lift them, the gussets will be put in place and new rivets will be installed. Newer bridges don't use rivets any longer. Your father found a company that still makes them."

Her father had unlocked a storage bin and found some boxes of large rivets inside. He chose a few rivets to take with him and locked the bin. Then he walked over to where Ann and Bruce were looking at the gussets.

"I want to test these back at the lab." He said, holding up the rivets. "I was told that they didn't round over very well so I'll make certain that the makeup of the metal is correct, and I also need to test their tensile strength while I'm at it."

Mr. Jenkins said, "I bet it's just because the guys haven't ever used rivets to connect steel before. You really have to heat them up properly before you round them over."

"I hope you're right, Bruce, but I need to make sure that these are correct for the job."

"Okay Andy, thanks for checking. Let me know what you come up with. I'll be going to go over the proper way to install rivets with the guys, too."

Ann listened to all the conversation, understanding some of it, deciding to save her questions for later.

"Okay, Bruce. Thanks for showing Ann this stuff. We will head out of here now. It was good to see you."

"Yep, you too. Say, will you be here on Monday?"

"Maybe late in the day. I have a lot to do back in the office."

"All right then. I'll lock up the gate behind you. It was nice to meet you, Ann." Bruce smiled and waved to Ann and Andy as they got into their car. They waved back, and then turned the car back the way they had come in and toward the highway.

The dirt road turned the left and they drove through the gate they had entered minutes before. Soon they were back on the highway with real pavement under them. There was also plenty of traffic.

"Are you hungry, Ann?"

"Yes, how long before we can get home?"

"It will be a while. Why don't you and I stop someplace and get our lunch?"

Ann had never eaten away from home unless it was lunch at school or having a holiday meal at a relative's house. This would be a new experience and she felt both excited and a little scared.

"Where will we eat?"

"There is a little diner on our way. We are almost there."

Ann was about to ask what a diner was when Andy started to pull off the road and into a parking lot in front of a long building that looked something like a long bus or railroad car with a large sign on the front of the roof that said 'Dunkleberger's Diner' across it. The long building had windows all along the side and lots of shiny metal trim with light bulbs above the length of the windows.

Ann was fascinated with this place and was still staring at it from her seat as Andy came around to open her door to let her out.

She jumped down from the car and they walked through the door at the end of the diner. She saw that there was a long counter with stools on one side. Opposite that there were booths that ran along the windows.

A lady in a dress with a short skirt and an apron called out to them, "Sit anywhere, Sweetie."

Ann and her father chose a booth and perched themselves on the shiny red bench seats. Ann's chin just about made it above the table top which had an irregular pattern across it. It wasn't made of wood. It was like the plastic surface the tables in the school cafeteria had, only with a much more interesting pattern. At the edge by the window was a napkin holder with salt and pepper shakers on one side and red and yellow plastic bottles on the other, all held together by a chrome wire cage. Some menu cards were stuffed between that and the window. Andy reached

over and pulled out a couple of menus and gave one to Ann.

"Take a look at the menu, Princess, and see what you

would like to have for lunch."

Ann's eyes started reading the list under the large

word Lunch. She was looking for something that she

recognized and that she could eat with the gap from her

missing front teeth.

"What would you like to drink, Sweetie?" It was the

lady who wore the apron. She also had some kind of white

frilly thing on the top of her hair which looked like it was

going to drop out when she took a pencil out of her hair and

positioned it over a small pad of green paper.

"Milk for her and a coffee for me, please." replied Andy.

"Got it, Sweetie. I'll be right back."

"Do you see anything you might like, Princess?"

Ann was still trying to take it all in. Her eyes went back and forth over the menu. She didn't want to try anything tough to chew, but what? There were so many things to choose from, yet it looked as if it would all be impossible for her to eat with her two front teeth missing. Her heart was beating faster and she found the words on the menu start to flow all together. She knew that her father was looking at her expecting an answer. She could feel tears starting. No, she wasn't going to cry. She couldn't. Then she spotted some things she thought would work.

"I think a grilled cheese sandwich and some peach slices with cottage cheese."

"My goodness, Ann, that is the most creative lunch choice I have ever heard from you."

She peeked above her menu and saw that he was smiling and proud. She hid her own smile behind the menu in her hands.

The lady with the apron had returned with their drinks. She put the milk in front of Ann and the coffee in front of Andy.

"Do you need any cream for that coffee?"

"No, thank you," said Andy.

"Well, what can I get you two then?"

She looked at Ann who still held the menu in front of her mouth.

"I would like a grilled cheese sandwich and some peach slices with cottage cheese." Which actually came out sounding like: "I would like a gwilled sheez sanwish wiff sum peash slieshes wiss cottag sheez."

The lady smiled and wrote on her pad of paper and then looked to Andy.

"I would like a ham sandwich with chips and a pickle, please."

"Do you want the bread toasted?"

"Sure."

"You got it, Sweetie," she said and stuck her pencil back in her hair as she turned around and headed behind the counter.

Ann put down her menu and turned to see where the apron lady had gone. The lady was taking pages from the green pad and stuck them on a large spinning thing that looked sort of like a merry-go-round. A guy behind a big open window spun the merry-go-round so he could look at the green pieces of paper. Then he disappeared into the kitchen behind the window.

"So, Ann, do you have any questions?"

Ann turned back to her father.

"What are rivets, Daddy?"

"It's an older way of connecting pieces of metal together. Today we would use bolts and washers or even weld two pieces of metal together with great heat. Welding melts pieces of metal so that they join each other as if they were one piece. Bolts and nuts need a hole to go through and then they must be tightened so that they clamp the metal pieces and won't come loose. In the past a very hot rivet would be put through a hole to join two pieces of metal. One end of the rivet has a large kind of hat on it so it won't pull through the hole and the other end is pounded over to make a hat on the other side so it can't pull out."

"Why do you use it if it is an old way to join metal?"

"The bridge is an old design that used rivets. Rivets allow the bridge parts to move and flex a little. If I used other methods the bridge parts could lose their flexible nature and start to crack instead of holding together. The steel that was made when the bridge was first constructed is different from the steel that I would be able to get today if I was making the bridge from scratch. So I had to think like the original bridge designer did and plan how to strengthen it without having to make a whole new bridge. The gussets won't make the bridge weigh that much more, but will allow it to take a lot more traffic."

"But Daddy, those metal gussets are very heavy. I couldn't lift them and neither could Mr. Jenkins."

"Yes, they are, Princess, although compared to the weight of the whole bridge they are very light."

Ann screwed up her face as she tried to understand what her father had just said.

"Here, let me show you something…"

Andy unrolled the paper ring from around the napkin that held their knife and fork. He stood the rectangular strip of paper on its thinnest edge and then put his coffee cup on the top edge. The piece of paper collapsed under the weight of the coffee cup. Then he lifted the coffee cup and made the piece of paper into a ring like it had been when it was surrounding the napkin and stuck it to itself. It was standing on the thin edge again. This time when he placed the coffee cup on top, it held up all the weight without collapsing.

"Sometimes, when things are the right shape, they have a great deal of strength for their weight. When the piece of paper wasn't connected to itself it could not

support any weight at all. When I made it into a ring it was

connected and it borrowed strength from itself so it could

hold up a lot of weight. The bridge is the same way. It uses

a lot of triangles to keep itself from falling down because

they are all tied together helping each other. If it was one

solid piece of metal it would be strong but weigh too much

to stay up. The paper ring has a huge hole in it and weighs

very little. It could also be a solid piece of metal and hold a

lot of weight too, but it would weigh a lot more. So we got

rid of all the unnecessary weight and just kept what was

needed to hold up the coffee cup. The bridge has a lot of

gaps in it as it is made of a lot of open triangles. I found that

if we just reinforced the pointy parts of the triangles they gain enough strength to carry four times the traffic that it can now."

Just then the food arrived and the lady with the apron placed each of their orders in front of them.

"Do you need anything else, Sweetie?"

"I think we're all set, thank you'" said Andy.

"If you need anything just give me a wave." The waitress smiled and scooted off to another table.

Chapter 5

Ann and her father enjoyed their meal at the diner.
Ann asked more questions about the bridge project and
what her father did all day. She learned that he spent a lot
of his day in meetings and on the phone. He also had to find
time to do actual design work that involved the bridge
project as well as other projects, which was often the reason
he arrived home late.

They finished their lunch and the lady with the apron
came over to check on them.

"Does anyone have room for dessert?" she asked.

Ann shook her head. She had filled up on the grilled
cheese sandwich and the peaches were kind of a sweet

dessert for her. She also remembered that they had a pair

of apples in a bag in the car.

"I guess that will be it," said Andy.

"You two have a wonderful day then." The lady put a

piece of paper near Andy's plate and walked off to help

another customer.

Andy looked the check over and dug some money out

of his pocket. He left a couple of dollar bills on the table and

then, motioning to Ann, got up and headed over to a cash

register at the end of the long counter with stools in front of

it. He and Ann stood in front of it and a cashier took the

piece of paper from Andy.

She told Andy the total of the bill and he pulled his wallet out of his hip pocket and handed her some money from it. There was a dinging sound from the cash register and the drawer opened. The cashier put the money that Andy had given her in the drawer and then pulled out a couple of dollar bills and some change and handed it back to him.

"Thank you, come again," she said cheerfully.

Ann and her father went outside and back into the car.

As Andy got Ann in her seat and belted in she asked, "What did you put the money on the table for Daddy?"

"That's called a gratuity or tip. When you eat out someplace you pay for your meal and then leave a little extra for the person that waits on you."

"Why is that?"

"That is how they make their money. The restaurant pays them a little for working there. If they do a really good job helping the customers they make much more from tips."

Ann thought about that.

"Do you get tips where you work?"

"No, Princess, I get paid a salary so I don't get any tips," Andy smiled.

"What is celery? I thought it was a vegetable?"

Andy laughed, "No Dear, I said _salary_. You are correct, celery _is_ a vegetable. Salary is how a person gets paid to work. Some people are paid by the number of hours they work and that is called wages. Others are paid a set amount and that is called salary."

Her father went around to the driver's side and got in the car. He was just putting it in reverse when rain drops started hitting the windshield.

Chapter 6

Andy backed the car out of its parking space and turned on the windshield wipers.

They made their way back onto the highway heading home. The rain picked up in its intensity, making louder tapping noise as it splattered against the glass. Soon the road was shiny and wet with more and more water.

Ann had never had the view of the road that she had now. Before, all she could do was look out the side windows and mostly in an up direction. Now she could see way off in the distance. As more rain came down it got harder and harder to see. The roads were very wet. The cars were starting to slow down. It was getting darker as clouds obscured the sun. Her father turned on the car's lights and the windshield wipers.

"Are we going to be all right, Daddy?"

"Of course, Princess, I will just drive slower so we don't aquaplane."

"Airplane?"

"No, aquaplane. That's what happens when water from the rain gets between the tires and the road. Aqua is another way to say water. If the tires have too much water to go through or we travel too fast the tires will be lifted off the road and we can skid or spin."

"That sounds scary!"

"That's why I am driving slower, Princess. When there is water on the road it also takes longer to brake and slow the car down so I am trying to keep my distance from other cars."

Then the rain became less and less. In a few minutes it was just a few drops and the sun started to come out. Andy was able to turn off the windshield wipers.

"Oh, look at that, Princess!"

"What is it Daddy?"

"Off there, in the distance. Can you see the rainbow?"

Ann looked way off in the distance and saw a beautiful arch of colors that seemed to float out in front of them.

"Wow! That's beautiful! Where did that come from?"

"The sun is behind us and the rain is in front of us so the sunlight is refracted into different wave lengths and we see that as a ring of colors."

"What is refracted?"

"Well, you know what reflected means? A reflection comes right back to our eyes like a mirror does. Almost the same thing happens with refraction. The sunlight goes through a rain drop to its back side and is reflected back through the same rain drop. Only as it passes back through the water drop the light is slowed down and bent enough to separate out the different colors, which our eyes see as a rainbow."

"Wow. Oh look, it's gone now!"

"Yes, we can only see them when the conditions are right. We will be home in just a couple of more miles. You can tell your mother all about it."

Chapter 7

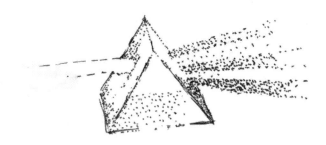

Soon they were at their house and her Dad pulled the car into the driveway. When it stopped her father came around and opened her door so she could jump to the ground. Buster was waiting for her wagging his tail as he danced excitedly by the car door.

"Hi, Buster, let's go inside."

Ann grabbed the bag containing the two apples to bring them back inside to the kitchen.

"You can leave them on the front seat and I'll take them into work Monday morning, Princess."

"Okay, Dad."

Ann and Buster walked up the front steps while her father moved the booster seat back to the rear of the car.

Her mother was in the front room playing on the piano and was singing a song about being by the sea shore. Ann and Buster went over to the upright piano. A Moment later her father joined them and sang along with his wife. Little Ann joined in, too. Soon even Buster wanted to sing along and howled with abandon.

Finishing up the song Ann's mother stopped playing and they all clapped for Buster. He wasn't quite sure what to do and he slowly wagged his tail as he looked at them for

a sign.

Andy petted Buster on the head and said, "Good boy!"

Ann gave Buster a hug and he wagged his tail harder.

Ann's mother asked, "So how was your adventure?"

Her father said, "Go ahead and tell your Mother what

we did, Princess."

Ann took a deep breath and said, "We went out to

where Daddy is making a bridge stronger and met Mr.

Jenkins. He is a man that works with Daddy. He showed me

the gussets that Daddy designed and how they will be put on

the bridge to make it stronger. Then we stopped for lunch

on our way home at a place called a diner. I read the menu

and picked out my own lunch. After lunch we drove home

and it was raining. When the rain stopped a rainbow

happened. Daddy said it was because of refraction. It was

beautiful Mommy."

"Oh my," said her mother, "that sounds like you had a

wonderful time."

"It was really fun, especially the rainbow."

"I have a way to make a rainbow here," said her Mom,

"Would you like to see?"

"Yes!"

Ann's mother took her by the hand and they went into

the kitchen together, with Andy and Buster following

behind. They went over to a drawer where Ann's mother

kept a collection of interesting things. She opened it and

poked around until she came up with a triangle of glass.

Then they went out the back door onto the porch. The glass

triangle was like a thick equilateral triangle. Ann's mother

found a spot on the porch rail where the sun was shining on

it and put down the glass triangle. Then she turned it so one

of the faces was toward the sun and on the other side she

put toward a piece of white paper that she had brought with

her. A tiny rainbow of colors appeared on the paper.

"Mom!" exclaimed Ann. "How did you do that?"

Her mother held up the glass triangle and said, "This is

a prism. The light that passes through it is bent and the

different colors in the light travel at different speeds

because the glass is thicker at the bottom than the top. The prism splits the separate colors out of the sun's light so you can see all the colors that regular light is made of. The different colors we see are called the light spectrum."

Ann thought about what her mother had just showed her. There were so many new things that she had learned today.

"Mom, how do you know all this stuff?"

Her mother smiled. "I always liked science and I went to college to study engineering. That is where your father and I met. We both studied engineering."

"How come you don't build things like Dad does?"

"I found that I liked music better. So I teach and play music. We have plenty of time left before it's supper time. What would you like to do with the rest of the afternoon?"

"I think I'll go out and sit under the tree in the back yard."

"Do you want to get a book?"

"No, I just want to sit under the tree."

"OK, Princess. Let me know if you need anything."

"Thanks Mom."

Ann went down the steps on the back porch and ambled over to the big tree in the back, picking one of the big roots that stuck out of the ground to sit on.

Chapter 8

Ann leaned against the tree and thought about all that
had happened that day. She had watched how her father
got the old bicycle from in the cellar working again and then
she watched how he replaced the fuel filter in their car.
Then she thought about how her mother had found a way to
turn her tangled hair into something wonderful.

Buster found Ann under the tree and came over to be
next to her. Ann rubbed him between the ears and on his
muzzle. Buster wagged his tail and put his head in her lap.

Ann thought about how different it was to ride up in
the front of the car on the booster seat. She saw so much
more of what was around them as the car drove to the work
site. It was the first time she had ever seen a place where

her father worked and seen the things that he did. Being able to eat lunch at the diner was also new to her. She was glad that she could read the menu by herself and figure out what to eat, but it had also been a little scary, too.

Seeing the rainbow had completely amazed her. It was so beautiful, and her mother knew all about them, too. She never knew that her mother had gone to college with her father either.

She looked down at Buster and pet him on his head.

"What am I going to do about you, Buster?"

Buster just wagged his tail some more and snuggled against her leg.

Ann thought about how her parents solved different problems and wondered if there was a problem of her own that she could solve. If she could only find a way to hang her clothes in the closet in her room _that_ would be a problem she would like to find a solution to. She thought about going inside and asking her mother if she had any ideas, but Ann really wanted to find a solution for herself. Maybe if she looked down in the cellar she might find something to solve her problem.

"Come on Buster, let's go inside."

Ann got up and went in the back door of the house and inside to the door to the cellar stairs. Her father and mother were working on the kitchen sink.

"Hi Mom," Ann said as she walked through the kitchen.

"Hi Honey, your Dad and I are trying to stop the kitchen sink's faucet from dripping. What are you up to?"

"I'm working on a problem, too. I need to see if there is something that I can use from the cellar."

"Do you need any help?"

"No, I don't think so, Mom."

"Okay, let me know if you do."

Ann opened the door to the cellar and peered down into the darkness. She had forgotten how dark it was down in the basement and tried to remember how her father had turned on the lights. Then she spotted the switch on the wall at the top of the stairs. She stretched out as far as she could, but wasn't able to reach it. She stepped down one step and tried again. Her finger just touched the switch plate when she made herself as tall as she could, but she was not tall enough to turn on the light. Ann sat down on the top step and put her elbows on her knees and her chin in her hands. She was caught between feeling angry and helpless. It wasn't fair. She looked up at the switch and thought to herself, "I hate you."

Buster had come over to her sensing that she needed some company and put his snout on her shoulder. Ann reached up and cuddled his head in her arm. Buster, loving the attention, wagged his tail. It knocked against the yardstick that was hanging on the kitchen wall. The clatter drew Ann's attention to the yardstick and an idea came to her.

"Buster, you are wonderful!" she exclaimed.

Ann got up and went over to the yardstick and lifted it off the hook. She then used it to push the light switch into the on position. She beamed with the pride of success and put the yardstick back on the hook. Now that the light was on in the basement she walked down the stairs to the bottom. Even with the lights on it was still dingy, with lots of shadows for things to hide in.

"Good grief," Ann said to herself.

Buster whined from the top of the stairs.

"It's okay boy."

Ann's eyes adjusted to the dim light and more things came into view. She wasn't really sure of what she was looking for, but there _were_ lots of things to see. There was a wooden work bench along one wall that had jars of screws, nails, and other metal things that she had no idea of what they were. Everything on the bench was covered with an oily dust. She looked around the other parts of the cellar and saw a couple of old wooden kegs, some saw horses, and some wooden planks leaning against a wall. Some old green screen doors were in another corner of the basement. Next to them was a broken rake and spade whose shovel blade was cracked and worn. There were some old wooden chairs shoved against a wall. Two of them were in pretty bad shape with one missing a leg and another with the spindles broken out of the back rest. The third one didn't appear to have any damage, but they were all very dusty.

Ann went back over to the bench and found a rag that she used to clean off the chair that looked the best. She couldn't find anything broken about it. She tested it out by sitting on its seat. It wiggled - a lot. She listened to the creaking sounds and discovered that there were spindles under the seat connecting to the legs that moved all over the place.

"Oh Dear, how do I fix _this_?"

Ann grabbed the loose spindles with her hands twisting and moving them around. She didn't have any idea how to fix them.

Up the stairs she went and found her mother alone in the kitchen.

"Mom?"

"Yes, Ann?"

"I need some help. Is Dad around?"

"He went to get some parts for the kitchen faucet. He could be a while. Is there anything I can help you with?"

"I've found a chair in the basement that I'd like to use, but it's all wiggly. I don't know how to fix it."

"Let me take a look and maybe we can figure out a solution together."

The two of them went down the stairs and Ann showed her mother the chair that she had chosen. Her mother looked it over carefully and took hold of the legs and spindles. Like Ann, she discovered that the joints were all loose.

"See Mom, it's all wiggly."

"I think we need to re-glue the joints, "Ann's mother said.

"Do we have glue?" asked Ann.

"We have different kinds of glue, but we will need glue that is made to work with wood. Let me look around down here and see if there is any. We will also need something to clamp and hold the chair tight together while the glue dries."

Ann's mother went over to the bench and looked through all the cans and boxes. It was a mess of clutter that was dusty and dirty. Eventually she found a metal can with a label that said it was wood glue.

"Aha!" she exclaimed, "This should do the trick, if it is still good."

She looked around the bench again and found a screw driver in the small tool box. She used the flat blade to pry the top off the metal canister. Then she peered inside and gently shook the can.

"This looks like it is still good."

She put the top back on the can and started looking around the cellar.

"What are you looking for now, Mom?"

"I need to find some rope or some straps that we can use to hold the chair tightly together after we put the glue on the joints."

"Would this work?"

Ann held up a small coil of rope that had been in one of the nail kegs. She had found it earlier when she was exploring the basement for a chair.

"That should be perfect! Now, can you find a small stick or piece of wood? It should be about a foot long."

Ann went back to the planks that she had seen leaning up against the wall earlier. She didn't find any short pieces of wood there so she went to look in back of the old screen doors. Again she didn't find anything.

"Hello!" Ann's father called from the top of the stairs.

"Hi honey, we're down here working on a project of Ann's."

"I'm back with a kit that should fix the leaking faucet."

"Do you need me up there to help you, Dear?"

"No, I don't think so. It should take me about twenty minutes or so."

Ann's mother opened the can of glue and then put the cover back on loosely.

"Ann, why don't we bring the chair up to the back porch and work on it out there in the sunshine? Here, I'll get the chair if you would carry up the rope and this can of glue."

Ann got the can and the rope while her mother grabbed the chair and they both climbed the stairs to the kitchen. Her father was on his back under the sink working on the faucet. She got ahead of her mother and held the screen door open for her.

"We will need to clean the wooden joints before we put the glue on," said her mother. "I'll need some sandpaper for that. I think I saw some down in the cellar."

Ann was looking in the can of glue.

"How come this glue is a powder?"

"We will need to add water and mix it up before we use it. I still need a good sized stick. Why don't you look around the back yard and see if you can find a strong stick or small branch?"

Ann went down the porch steps to look around and Buster decided to join her. She poked around the base of the big tree and the bushes around the edge of their yard. She tried a couple of sticks that ended up breaking too easily. Then she found a large tree branch that was plenty strong. The problem was that it was still a large branch and not practical to use unless she could find a way to shorten it up. Buster was busy checking out each of the sticks that Ann had rejected.

Ann's mother returned with some sandpaper from the basement and was checking on Ann's progress.

"What have you found, Princess?"

"Most of what I found is too small and weak, but there is a strong branch over here, it's just too long. I think."

"Let me take a look at what you have found," said her mother, "Say that *is* a good one. I bet I know where a saw is that we can use to shorten it up. You wait here and I'll go find it. I'll be back in a minute."

Ann went over to where Buster was. He had a stick in his mouth and was shaking his head all over the place.

"Grrrr," he said as he thrashed about with the stick. Then he dropped it on the ground and barked at it.

"Easy there, Buster," said Ann.

He looked up at her and she went over and patted him on his head.

"Here we go," Ann's mother said as she walked up with a hand saw.

She put the big branch on her knee and put the saw's teeth about a foot from the end. She started with a couple of short strokes and then used almost the length of the saw as she cut through the branch leaving a small pile of sawdust on the ground beneath her cut. In a few seconds she was almost through. Then she made a couple of quick, sharp thrusts that finished the job and the foot-long section fell to the ground.

Buster immediately grabbed the piece of wood off the ground and ran across the yard with it.

Ann's mother laughed and told Ann to see if she could get the stick away from the dog while she returned the saw to the basement.

Ann ran around the yard and Buster enjoyed staying just out of reach. Finally he dropped the stick and barked at Ann, giving her a chance to pick it up.

"Yuck," said Ann. The stick was all covered with his slobber.

Ann made a face as she walked with the stick back to the porch. Buster was excitedly jumping after her, barking and making grabs at the stick.

"Stop it, Buster!"

He calmed down just a bit and went from jumping to just a slow trot.

Ann's mother came out of the kitchen with a small paper cup and a single chopstick. She sat down on the porch bench and turned the old chair over so she could get to the loose spindles. She then took a small piece of sandpaper and cleaned each end as well as the holes that the spindles had come out of. Ann watched as her mother carefully sanded each one.

"Ann, I need you to get a little water in this paper cup for me. Go in and see if your father has got the kitchen sink working yet. If he has, put some water in the cup, but just a little water."

126

"Okay, Mom."

Ann took the cup inside to the kitchen sink.

"Are you done yet, Dad?"

"Just about, Princess, I've got to pick up my tools and put them away, but the faucet shuts off without dripping now."

"Would you put a little water in this cup for me, Dad?"

Her father took the cup and put it under the faucet filling it about a quarter of the way from the bottom.

"Is that enough?"

"I think so, Dad."

"What are you going to do with it?"

"Mom is making some wood glue so we can fix the wobbly chair."

"That should be enough water then. She can always pour out some if it's too much."

"Thanks, Dad."

Ann returned to her mother and showed her the cup of water.

"Is that enough, Mom?"

"Plenty, I'll just put in some of this wood glue powder and mix it with the water."

She stirred the powder into the water with the wooden chop stick and it turned a light brown color. She added a little bit more powder and stirred it some more.

"That should do it!"

"Now what, Mom?"

"We coat the parts of the wood that we want to glue and then assemble them together."

She used the chopstick to put glue on the ends of the spindles and then into each hole, assembling the chair spindles and legs as she went. Soon it was all together.

"Ann, where is that rope you found in the cellar?"

"Right here, Mom."

"I'm going to need your help with this, Ann. As I wrap the rope around the legs I need you to keep it from falling off until I can get it tight."

"Okay."

The rope was wrapped around the legs at the same height as the spindles and Ann made sure that it stayed up as her mother circled the chair legs with it. Then her mother brought the ends together with a simple knot.

"Now hold this until I can attach the stick we cut."

Ann kept the rope from slipping down and her mother placed the stick at the knot and then tied another knot over the stick.

"As I twist this stick it will tighten up the legs."

Sure enough, the rope got tighter as her mother spun the stick slowly. When it was tight enough her mother tied the stick to the leg with a small piece of twine so it could not spin loose. Her mother put her hand on the chairs seat and put some pressure on it to see how tight it was. The chair didn't wobble a bit.

"There!"

"Mom, that's amazing!"

"We will have to let it dry overnight, but by tomorrow morning the glue will be dry and the chair will be sturdy again. Let's carefully bring it inside so it will be protected."

Her mother picked up the chair and Ann ran forward to hold the door open for her.

"I'll put it in the front room where it will be safe."

So into the front room went the repaired chair. Ann stared at it with a smile on her face. She hated that she had to wait until tomorrow to start using it. Then, with a big sigh she turned and went back out to the porch.

"What do we do now, Mom?"

"I've got to put these things away and we've got to put the rest of this glue that I mixed up somewhere safe so it can harden before we throw it away."

She followed her mother to the basement where the can of powdered glue was put back on the shelf and the chopstick was taken out of the small paper cup. Her mother wiped off the glue from the stick and put it on the bench sticking out of a glass jar. Then she put the paper cup on the bench.

"We've got to make sure that the cat and dog don't get down here. I don't want them messing around with this stuff."

Up the stairs they went again. Her mother turned off the light and closed the door to the cellar with a click. She tried the handle to make certain it was shut. It was.

"Now, how about helping _me_ with supper?"

Chapter 9

Ann and her mother worked together to get the supper ready. The two of them prepared some potatoes for mashing by peeling and boiling them. Ann washed and peeled the potatoes while her mother got some water boiling. Her mother prepared some chicken as the main part of the meal. She removed the skin and bones and then coated them with a mix of flour and bread crumbs. Next was a vegetable, and Ann's mother picked out some Brussel sprouts that would be steamed. The oven was set to heat up for baking the chicken and then Ann's mother prepared the Brussel sprouts by cutting them up into quarters. She had a pot with a basket in it so that water would be heated into steam and she would cook them that way.

There was nothing left for Ann to do, so she went back into the front room to check on how the chair was coming along.

Ann ran her hand over the chair and checked on how tight the rope was. She was excited to see her solution coming together and wished that she could use the chair already.

"Ann, could you come help me with the potatoes?"

"Be right there, Mom."

Ann returned to the kitchen. Her mother had a bowl filled with the potatoes that had been sliced up and boiled.

"Here is the potato masher, Ann. See what you can do to get them mashed up while I work on the chicken and the vegetable."

Ann sat in a chair with the bowl in her lap and mashed away. The potatoes had become nice and soft so it wasn't too hard a job to mash them up. It did take a while, though. Ann's mother hummed a tune as she went about the final preparations. The steam pot was boiling and the Brussel sprouts had been dropped into the steam basket.

Ann's mother cracked open the oven to take a peek at the chicken. A wonderful smell rose out of the oven.

"I think everything is just about ready. How are you coming with the mashing?"

"Pretty good, Mom, take a look."

Ann's mother looked at the potatoes in the bowl and with a smile took the bowl and placed it on the counter, added a little butter and milk, and did some final mashing.

"Go see if you can find your father and tell him that dinner is ready, will you Ann?"

Ann got off her chair and headed into the front room. No one was there so she went up the stairs to check her parent's bedroom. She opened the bedroom door a crack and saw that her father had fallen asleep on the bed. She went over and shook him by his shoulder.

After a couple of good shakes his eyes fluttered open.

"Hey, did I fall asleep?"

"Dad, Mom has supper ready."

Her father rubbed his eyes and sat on the side of the bed.

"Let her know that I'll be right down, Princess. I'll just wash my hands. What are we having? It smells delicious!"

"Baked chicken and mashed potatoes. I'll go down and let her know."

Ann headed back down the stairs and into the kitchen.

"Dad's coming, Mom. He was asleep, but he is washing his hands and will be right down."

"Wonderful. You wash yours and then set the table and I'll get the food onto the dishes."

Ann put out cloth placemats, napkins, and then the forks and knives on the kitchen table. By the time she had that done her father had arrived in the kitchen.

"Anything I can do to help?" he asked.

"Would you pour a glass of milk for Ann? I'd like some water and you can get yourself whatever you want. I have just about everything on the plates so go ahead and sit down when you're ready."

Ann sat down at her place and her father got out glasses and poured everyone's beverage. As Andy sat down Ann's mother put a plate of delicious food in front of each of them.

"Brussel sprouts," exclaimed her father. "I love them."

Ann's mother smiled.

They started eating. Ann liked the mashed potatoes because they tasted great and was easy to chew, the chicken smelled terrific, too. She took her knife and cut the chicken into some smaller pieces to make them easier to eat. Like her father, she loved Brussel sprouts.

"So what was everyone's favorite part of the day?" Andy asked.

"I liked playing the piano and working some more on my song," Ann's mother said.

"I liked getting the chair fixed so I can use it in my room tomorrow," exclaimed Ann.

"And what will you do with it in your room?" Andy asked.

"It's a surprise. I'll show you tomorrow," said Ann, with a mischievous smile.

"Aha, a mystery! I can't wait for the surprise." Andy smiled.

"So what was your favorite part of the day, Daddy?"

"My goodness, there are so many things to choose from. I was glad to solve the problem with the car and the kitchen sink, but I think being able to spend the morning with you, Princess, was pretty special."

They soon finished their dinner and Ann's mother brought out a desert of strawberry ice cream with some whipped cream on top. Ann finished her desert and asked to be excused. Then she went back to the front room while her parents cleaned up the dishes.

Ann ran her hands over the chair again and checked that the rope was nice and tight. Duster had jumped up on the seat and was taking another one of her naps. Ann rubbed Duster's ears and the cat stretched out and savored the attention.

Ann started humming the song her mother had sung earlier in the afternoon. She thought about the words of the song and imagined how it would be to be by the sea and hear the wind and waves that the song talked about. She wondered if there would be rocks or sand by the ocean, or would there be grass and trees.

"Princess, would you like to play some cards tonight?"

It was her Dad who had come into the front room while she was humming.

"Gee, Dad, I don't think so. Would Mom be able to read us a story?"

"That's a great idea, let me go ask her."

In a few seconds her parents had joined Ann in the front room.

"What story would you like to hear tonight Ann?" her mother asked.

"I don't know, you pick it out, Mom."

"I'll do that. In the mean time you and your father get comfortable on the couch while I check the book case for something that we can all enjoy."

Andy sat at one end of the couch and Ann sat next to him. Buster jumped up next to Ann and snuggled against her, putting his muzzle on her leg. Ann's mother returned with a well-worn book and sat down opposite them in a wing-back chair. There was a floor lamp over her right shoulder that cast light on her lap and provided the perfect illumination for her to read by. Duster soon jumped up and squeezed herself between the chair and Ann's mother's leg.

Ann's mother's reading voice was as melodious as her singing voice and soon Ann's head was full of images of a time long ago when a young boy and his mother ran an inn near the sea. A strange old sailor rented a room from them and soon they were visited by a creepy one-eyed man who left a strange piece of paper for the old sailor. It had a black dot on the paper and that scared the old sailor nearly to death. The young boy found some mysterious papers in the old sailor's sea chest and then someone came and killed the old sailor. There were more descriptions of pirates and a good doctor, but Ann's eyelids were getting heavy and she soon fell asleep curled up next to her father and Buster.

Chapter 10

It was morning and Ann woke up to the sound of birds chirping and sunlight streaming in her window. She slowly opened her eyes and looked out the window. Squirrels were chasing each other about the branches of the tree outside in the yard.

She was sorting out memories of pirates and treasure when she realized that her chair must be ready. She jumped out of bed and headed down the stairs to the front room. There was the chair with the rope still tight around the legs. She ran her hands across the seat and tested how stable the chair was. It was nice and sturdy.

"Is that you, Ann?"

It was her mother calling from the kitchen. Her mother walked from there to the front room. She had her apron on and her hair was gathered into a bun.

"It looks good, doesn't it?"

"It looks wonderful, Mom."

"See if you can get your father down here for breakfast, and you come down, too. I bought some fresh eggs yesterday so we will have scrambled eggs. I baked some bread as well. Now scoot and we will get your chair ready after we have breakfast."

"Aw, Mom, I've been waiting all night!"

"I know, Princess, but we need to eat our breakfast. Now please go get your father for me."

"Okay."

Ann climbed the stairs and headed to her parents' bedroom but discovered that her father was in the bathroom shaving. The bathroom door was open and Ann watched as he finished using a brush to cover his lower face and neck with white shaving cream. Then he took a razor and scraped his neck with the blade and rinsed off the lather in the sink.

"Hi, Daddy, Mom wants us to come down for breakfast. I want to get my chair and bring it up to my room."

Andy paused, "I will just be a couple of minutes and then I will head right down. I'll help you with your chair after breakfast, if you want."

"Does it hurt when you shave?"

"Not if you do it right."

"Do you have to shave?"

"No, I could grow a beard, but I would rather shave. Maybe someday I'll grow a mustache."

"Oh, Daddy, that would be wonderful!"

By that time he had managed to finish shaving in between questions and took a warm, wet, washcloth and cleaned his face. He wrung out the excess water, took a look at his face, and hung it up.

"Let's head down and get our breakfast, Princess."

The two of them headed back down the stairs, as they went by the front room, Ann paused for another look at her chair.

"See, Daddy?"

"It looks great. Let's go eat."

On they went to the kitchen.

"My, doesn't your father look handsome?"

Ann's mother went over and gave her father a big hug and a quick kiss. Ann rolled her eyes and sighed.

They sat down to a lovely breakfast of scrambled eggs, toast, and orange juice.

"When did we get the orange juice?" Andy asked.

"While you two were having your adventures yesterday I walked down to the corner grocery store and picked up a few things. They had just gotten in some oranges from Florida. Mr. Simms told me that they were honey bells and were perfect for juice so I bought a dozen. I was able to get a couple of dozen eggs, too."

Ann ate her breakfast as quickly as she could. She was anxious to get to her chair. She left the crust of her toast uneaten as it was hard for her to chew. Other than that her plate was clean and she was squirming with excitement.

"Can I go to my chair now?"

"Yes, you may, Princess. Your father and I will have some coffee and be right in."

Ann jumped down and ran into the front room. She looked at the rope and tried to figure out how to get it undone so she could release the chair. The stick that was used to tighten the rope was itself tied to a chair leg with some twine. Ann looked at it and saw that it was tied in a bow like she tied her shoe laces. She found the ends and pulled them to undo the bow. Once that was done the stick started unwinding and the loosened rope fell to the floor.

Ann checked the chair again by pushing sideways on the seat. The chair didn't wiggle or squeak. It was done!

"Well, look at you, Ann; you've got it all undone by yourself!"

"It's perfect, Mom, it doesn't wiggle or anything. Thanks for helping me get it fixed."

Andy walked into the room and smiled at the sight of Ann having released her chair from the rope.

"Now will you show me what you are going to do with your chair, Princess?"

"Sure, Daddy, first I need to bring it up to my room."

"I can give you a hand with that if you'd like. We can clean up the rope and stuff later."

Andy bent down and grabbed the chair. He and Ann walked up the stairs to her room and Andy put it down near her bed. Ann took hold of the chair and slid it over to her closet, climbed up on the seat and stood up high. She could finally reach the clothes hanger in her closet!

"Look, Daddy, I can use my closet now!"

"Well, what do you know, I never realized that you couldn't do that. It looks like you will need some more clothes hangers, young lady."

"Do we have some?"

"I will take a look around. In the mean time you go get your Mom and show her what you've done. I think that she will be quite impressed."

Ann jumped down from the chair and headed back down the stairs only to find her mother coming up them.

"What's all the excitement?"

"Mom, take a look at what I've done."

Ann's mother accompanied Ann into her bedroom and watched while Ann climbed back onto the seat of the chair and demonstrated how she could now reach the closet rod and the single hanger that dangled from it.

"My goodness, Ann, that's wonderful! How did you think of that?"

Her mother looked down at the boxes of Ann's clothes on the floor next to the bed.

"Oh my, we need to wash those clothes before you hang them up. What will we do for more hangers?"

"I'm going to see if we have any more in the house." Ann's father turned and started exploring the closets upstairs and down.

Ann's mother gathered up the boxes of clothes and headed downstairs to the kitchen where the clothes washer was. Ann followed along, not sure whether to see what her father could find or to help her mother. Eventually she went in the kitchen and watched as her mother filled the washing machine with her clothes.

"I had no idea that your clothes were getting so full of cat hair!"

"And dog hair, too, Mom. They like to sleep in the boxes at night."

Ann's mother started the washer. Just then Andy came in to announce that all he was able to come up with was one additional clothes hanger.

"This is all I could find, but I have an idea. I'll take a walk down to City Dry Cleaners and see if they might have some."

"Will they be open today, Dear?"

"Oh, that's right, it's Sunday. Well, maybe I can get lucky or maybe I can think of something else. It's worth a try anyway. I will be back in a few minutes. Wish me luck."

Andy disappeared out the door while Ann's mother filled the washing machine with clothes and added some detergent. When she switched it on the washing machine started to add water and wash the clothes.

"Come on, Ann; let's clean up the front room. The rope is still on the floor."

She and Ann went into the front room and picked up the rope, the stick, and the twine. Her mother showed Ann how to coil rope so that it wouldn't become all twisted and took the twine to hold the coil together so that they could hang the rope down in the cellar. While they were down there, her mother found the paper cup they had used yesterday with the leftover glue in it. The glue had dried solid. They took the cup of glue and threw it away in the kitchen waste basket.

"It will be a while before the wash is done, let's get out the vacuum cleaner and vacuum the house."

The vacuum cleaner was kept in a closet in the kitchen. It was a big can on wheels with a long hose and tube with a wide end for cleaning the floors. Ann's mother brought it up stairs and started vacuuming her own bedroom. Then she moved to Ann's room where she spent extra time getting up a lot of cat and dog hair before she moved on the hall and the stairs. She unplugged the vacuum cleaner so she could work her way down the stairs before starting at the front of the house. Ann helped he mother by pushing furniture out of her way and then pushing it back in place. When that was done the kitchen was the last place to get vacuumed. With the house done the vacuum cleaner was unplugged and the cord was wrapped around the machine before it was put away in the closet.

"Look what I found!"

It was Andy with a handful of metal clothes hangers.

"Daddy, where did you find them?"

"I got lucky. Your Mom was right, the place was closed, but Amy, the woman that runs the place, was working in the back of the shop getting things ready for tomorrow. She recognized me and I told her what I was looking for and why. She went and found a large handful of hangers that she said they were going to throw out," He said with a smile.

The washing machine was starting its final spin cycle. That would get most of the water out of the clothes that it had just rinsed. Ann's mother had a wicker basket to put the clothes in along with some clothes pins so they could hang them on the clothesline in the back yard. Andy and Ann took the clothes hangers up to her room and Ann hung them in her closet in readiness for her soon-to-be clean clothes.

By the time they were back downstairs the washing machine had finished spinning the clothes and her mother was transferring the clothes from the machine to the wicker basket.

"Ann, give me a hand with hanging the clothes, please."

"Okay, Mom."

Ann and her mother went out into the back yard where a clothesline was strung between a two posts with a board across their tops that made them look like the letter "T". The clothesline went back and forth from one T to the other. Ann handed her mother clothespins one at a time so that she could attach the clothes to the line. It was a sunny day with a light breeze so it would not be long before the clothes would be dry.

All this time Buster and Duster had been trying to figure out where their boxes had gone. Duster had finally ended up finding a place in one of the downstairs windows that had some morning sun. Buster had spent his time following Ann and her mother around until they pulled out the vacuum cleaner. He didn't like the noise it made so he found a place to take a nap under the big old tree in the back yard. He did open an eye to watch them when they started to hang the clothes on the line, but then went to sleep.

Chapter 11

Ann and her mother were in the front room. Her mother was playing the piano and writing music. She would play a few notes and then stop to write them down. Ann was sitting on one end of the piano bench watching the process. As the morning warmed up her father had opened the windows that had screens so that a breeze would blow through the house making things feel fresh and clean. Her father lay down on the couch to read the newspaper only to fall asleep a few minutes later.

"Mom, do you think that I could learn to play the piano?"

"Of course you can. Would you like to start now?"

"How long will it take?"

"It took me a lot of practice to play like I do now, but in the beginning I found I could play some simple things in just a little while."

"Oh, I wish I could play like you do."

"I wish you could too, Ann. It will take a while and at times you will find it frustrating, but if you keep at it you can become even better than me."

"Show me how to get started, Mom."

Ann's mother let Ann sit in the center of the piano bench and placed her fingers on the keys. She showed her the scale of "do, re, mi, fa, sol, la, ti, do" and then helped her get her own fingers to play the scale. Ann struggled as her fingers were short. Seeing her frustration, her mother showed her a simple tune that Ann could play with just a one finger of both hands. She called it Chopsticks. Ann loved being able to make music come from the piano. Then Ann's mother showed her how they could both play Chopsticks at the same time with a harmony of sound. Ann loved that they could play something together.

"Oh, Mom, this is fun!"

"I know that it's tough when your hands are small, but if you work at it you will find yourself getting better. I struggled at it when I was a little girl. My hands were little to start with, too."

"Really, Mom, but you are so tall and your fingers are long."

"I know Dear, we all change as we get older. You will see a lot of changes as you grow older, too."

"I hope so, Mom. I hate being so little."

"Life is full of change Ann. Learn to make the most of life now no matter what you think of your size. You can do and become whatever you want to in life. It won't always come fast or easy, but if it is a good thing, it will be worth whatever work you must put in to make it yours."

Ann sat there thinking about what her mother had just said.

"Princess, I think your clothes are dry by now. Let's go out back and get them off the clothesline."

Her mother got up from the piano and grabbed the wicker basket on their way out to the clothesline. Ann's mother took the clothes pins off and handed them to Ann as she folded each piece of clothing and she put them in the basket. Ann bent down and smelled her clothes. They had a wonderful smell of the wind and the sun. It was much better than the smell of Buster and Duster.

"Are you getting all the clothes pins?"

"Yes, Mom," Ann replied as she formed a basket with the bottom of her shirt to hold them all.

She followed her mother back in to the kitchen and dumped the pins into a pile on the kitchen table.

"I think I'll iron some of these dresses", said her mother.

"Can I help?"

"Of course, let me get out the ironing board and heat up the iron."

The ironing board was in the same closet as the vacuum cleaner and the iron was on a shelf in the closet. Ann's mother unfolded the ironing board and then put some water in the iron before plugging it in to heat up.

"Ann, pull one of the kitchen chairs over here so you can stand up tall enough to help me iron."

Ann dragged a chair over to the ironing board and stood up on it enjoying her new found height. Her mother wet her finger and quickly touched the bottom of the iron.

"It needs to heat up a little more."

Ann leaned over the ironing board and put her elbows down on it and put her chin in her hands. The board started rocking and the iron fell to the floor.

"Oh no!"

Ann's mother grabbed the iron off the floor and checked it to see if it was still working. Everything appeared to be fine.

"Careful, Ann, the ironing board is a little shaky."

"I'm sorry, Mom."

"That's okay, but it sure put a dent in the floor."

Ann looked down and saw a gouge in the linoleum from where the corner of the iron hit it.

"Are we in trouble, Mom?"

"I don't think so, Princess. This is an old house and this floor has seen a lot of things hit it over the years."

Ann looked around the kitchen at the floor and for the first time saw that it had quite a few little scars and a lot of wear. Ann's mother tested the iron again and this time it was hot enough to use.

"Now watch me and how I use the iron," Ann's mother said as she laid out one of Ann's dresses on the board and smoothed the cloth with the hot iron.

"I can't let the iron stay too long on the cloth or it will start to burn it."

She moved the dress to a fresh surface again and again until she had ironed the whole thing. Then she took it off the board and held it up to Ann.

"There, this one is done. Why don't you take it upstairs and hang it in your closet while I'll work on the next piece."

Ann carefully got down from the chair and took her dress. She held it up as she climbed the stairs and headed to the closet in her room. Then she draped it on the back of the chair so she could use her arms to hoist herself up and stand on the chair's seat. Then she took one of the hangers and carefully hung the dress on it before placing it on the closet rod. She took a Moment to sniff the dress and inhale the smell of the ironed cloth. She smiled and felt so happy.

By the time she got back to the kitchen her mother was done with another piece and Ann took it up to her closet and hung that one up, too. Ann went back and forth as her clothes got ironed. Finally her mother handed her the last item and Ann took it upstairs to hang up, too.

When she returned to the kitchen her mother had something for Ann to practice ironing with.

"Here is a handkerchief that you can practice on," she told Ann.

Ann climbed up on the chair and her mother laid the handkerchief out on the ironing board. Ann lifted the iron to start to use it and found it very heavy. She tried to brace herself on the ironing board and panicked as it started wiggling. Her mother quickly steadied everything and helped Ann get started.

"Just move the iron back and forth until the handkerchief looks smooth."

Ann did so and the handkerchief flattened out. Ann stopped for a second and her mother quickly picked up the iron and set it on its end.

"Remember to keep the iron moving. If you need to stop it has to be rested on its end so it doesn't burn anything."

"I'm tired, Mom. I didn't know that the iron was so heavy!"

"It's heavy and hot. It takes a lot of work and concentration to use, but it makes your clothes look nice."

Her mother turned off the iron and unplugged it so it would cool off. She put the pieces of Ann's clothes, that wouldn't be hung up, back in one of the boxes that would sit on the floor next to her bed and handed them to Ann.

"Mom, how will I keep Buster and Duster from sleeping on these clothes?"

"Well, for now just put the empty box on top of the one with your socks and stuff. That way they will be protected if the cat or dog decides to sleep in the box. Maybe we can think of something better, but now I've got to put all this away and get our lunch made.

Ann made her way back up to her room with the boxes and thought about how she could find a better place for her clothes. Maybe she could look down in the basement again. There might be something else that she could use down there!

Chapter 12

While Ann thought about what she might find in the basement her mother was busy making lunch for the family. She had boiled some eggs that morning and now was slicing up some radishes and celery to make egg salad. Once the vegetables were prepared she chopped up the eggs and mixed the ingredients together with some mayonnaise. She sliced some fresh bread she had made and made sandwiches for everyone. She put a leaf of lettuce in each sandwich, too.

"All right everyone, lunch is ready!"

Ann was sitting in the front room watching to see if her father was going to wake up. When she heard her mother call she went over and shook her father's shoulder. He opened his eyes and seemed surprised.

"Did I fall asleep?"

"Yes, Dad, lunch is ready."

"Oh my goodness let your mother know that I'll be right there. I need to wash my hands and splash some cold water on my face."

Ann jumped off the chair and went into the kitchen.

"Dad will be right in. He needs to wash his hands."

"Well, I guess you should wash your hands, too, Princess. Use the stool and the kitchen sink. There's a towel hanging on the oven's handle."

Ann washed up and dried her hands and then headed for the kitchen table. Her father appeared and asked if there was anything he could do to help.

"Go ahead and get us each something to drink. Ann, is milk okay for you?"

"Sure, Mom."

They all sat down to a scrumptious lunch.

"So who let me sleep all morning?"

Ann and her mother laughed.

"You were tired, Dear," Ann's mother said.

After lunch Andy and Ann washed the dishes while her mother went in to the piano. The notes spread around the house filling it with a melody that brought a feeling of cheer to the whole family.

"So what are your plans for the afternoon, Princess?"

"I need to find a better place to put my clothes, Daddy."

"I thought you could use your closet now."

"That works for clothes that I can put on hangers, but I can't hang up everything I have. It needs to be something that Buster and Duster won't sleep in."

"Why don't we take a look in the cellar and see if there is anything that you can use? We just have a couple of plates left to clean."

Ann wondered if her father knew that she was thinking about looking in the cellar, too.

Ann and Andy finished up the last of the dishes and placed them on the drying rack. Ann hung the drying towel on the handle of the oven and wiggled off the stool she had been sitting on. Then she and her father went down in the cellar to see what might be down there that she could use.

"I don't remember seeing any dresser or bureau down here, Princess."

They explored around the bench as their eyes got used to the low level of light that the bare light bulbs gave off. Ann went to some of the darker corners where tools and old wooden containers had been piled. She looked at some wooden nail kegs, but she thought they would be something that Duster would find too attractive. She went to another corner near where the old boards were stacked. There were some old wooden crates with glass jars in them. The crates didn't have lids so she felt they were just as useless as the kegs.

"Ann, come take a look at this!"

Ann went over to where Andy was looking.

"What is it, Daddy?"

Andy was bending over a piece of furniture that looked quite odd. It had a couple of drawers, but they were facing up toward the ceiling.

"What is that?"

"It's an old wooden file cabinet. It was covered up by those old tarps. Come help me stand it up."

The two of them lifted the short cabinet onto its legs so that the drawers looked normal. The file cabinet had two drawers and Andy pulled them open one at a time. The top drawer just had a couple of empty folders in it, but the bottom drawer had folders with things in them. Andy pulled out the folders so they could look at their contents. There were some old letters and a bunch of photographs in the folders.

"We can put these in another container. They are probably something the landlord will want to keep."

"I found some wooden boxes over in the corner over there."

"Why don't you go get one and bring it here? I'll clean up the drawers."

"What should I do with all the jars in the boxes?"

"Oh, let me come over and help you with that."

They looked at the jars to see what they could do with them. They were old canning jars that someone had saved. Most of them were clear glass, but a couple of them were a lovely blue color.

"I think I can fit most of them into the other box if I pack them carefully. Then I'd like to take these ones with blue glass and put them upstairs where they can sit on a window sill in the kitchen. It would look nice to have the sunlight shine through them. That will free up one crate for storing the contents of the old file cabinet."

Andy rearranged the glass jars into the one crate and ended up with three jars with blue glass. He took them up to the kitchen and placed them on one of the wide window sills. The afternoon sun came through the window and cast a lovely blue light through the jars.

Then he went back down in the cellar and moved the contents of the old file cabinet to the empty wooden crate. He put the crate up on the wooden bench near the basement windows. While he was doing that Ann took a rag and wiped down the two-drawer file cabinet.

"We can leave out the drawers so I can wrestle the file cabinet up to your room. Do you think that you can handle bringing the drawers up to your room one at a time, Princess?"

"I think so, Daddy."

Andy pulled the drawers and set them on the floor so he could get a good grip on the file cabinet and brought it up to the kitchen and then to Ann's room. Ann followed with the first drawer and then went back for the second one. By that time Andy had found a place for the file cabinet in her closet and had put the first drawer in place. Ann handed him the second drawer and Andy slid it into the cabinet.

"There, what do you think, Princess?"

"It's wonderful, Daddy!"

Ann opened the top drawer and took her socks and other items from the box on the floor and placed them inside the file cabinet drawers. Then she looked back at the empty boxes that used to hold all her clothes.

"Shall I throw out those old boxes, Princess?"

"Oh no, Daddy, where will Buster and Duster sleep then? I need to find something to put in the boxes to make them comfortable, to sleep in."

"You should ask your mother if she has any ideas for that. I need to turn off the light in the basement and close up the door. I need to get some reading done so that I'm ready for work tomorrow."

Andy went downstairs and Ann went into the front room where her mother was still playing on the piano. Her mother had gone from playing to writing more of her music.

"Hi Ann, did you want to practice on the piano some more?"

"I'd like to, but I need your help with something first."

"What is it, Princess?"

"Now that my old clothes boxes are empty I need to put something in them so that Buster and Duster can still sleep in them."

"That's a great idea. Let's go see what I have that might work and I need to see what you and your father found for you to put your clothes in, too."

They first walked into the kitchen and took a peek in the closet there where Ann's mother had a bag of rags. There were a couple of old rags that would work in one of the boxes. Ann's mother scowled and rubbed her chin as she thought about other possibilities.

"I know! I have an old bath towel in the upstairs linen closet. It is starting to get frayed and I haven't moved it to the rag bag yet. You take these and I'll get the old towel from the upstairs."

Ann followed her mother up the stairs and to the linen closet where her mother searched for the old towel. After a bit she found it on the bottom of the pile.

"There, that's the one! We will put it in one box and take the rags that you brought and line the other one with them."

They did just that and placed the now pet-comfy boxes at the end of Ann's bed. Then Ann's mother took a look at the re-purposed file cabinet in the clothes closet.

"My goodness, that's perfect Ann. You two were so fortunate to have found that cabinet!"

"Daddy found it for me. It was down in the cellar. It had some old papers and photos in it so we put those in another old wooden box and Daddy found some beautiful blue glass jars and put them in a kitchen window."

"Ann you have certainly accomplished a lot today. Tonight we will get your hair put up and looking nice for tomorrow when you go back to school. You only have a couple of weeks before it will be summer break. How about we go downstairs and practice on the piano?"

"Okay, Mom."

Ann and her mother spent the rest of the afternoon on the piano. Ann would practice for a while and then her mother would work on her music composition. Then Ann would practice some more. By late afternoon Ann had made a lot of progress. It even surprised her mother.

Even though Ann's fingers were short she found she could compensate by moving her arms more and holding her elbows higher. Her arms got tired, but she was now able to play more than "Chopsticks". She could play "Happy Birthday" and "Twinkle, Twinkle, Little Star." She could tell that her mother was very proud of her accomplishment. Ann was tired and she was happy.

That evening Andy made the supper for the family. It was spaghetti, a favorite of Ann's. After supper Ann took a bath and her mother fixed her hair with the brush that didn't hurt. It would still need some work the next morning, but it was good enough to sleep on.

Buster and Duster found their boxes to sleep in and settled in for the night.

Chapter 13

In the morning Ann had her breakfast and then brushed her teeth (wishing that she still had her two front ones) and put on her freshly ironed clothes. Her mother got Ann's hair looking better than ever and Andy exclaimed how good she looked. Ann was so happy she smiled broadly forgetting to try and hide her missing teeth.

She anxiously waited in front of the house for the school bus to arrive. Buster was sitting next to her on the front steps while she rubbed his head and around his ears.

With a squeal the bus came to a stop and Ann stepped up its steps and on to her seat. She could tell that the other children were looking at her. No one was calling her names, but they were surprised at how she looked.

In a few minutes the bus arrived at the school and Ann got off and walked to her classroom. She could hear that there were whispers going on around her as she took her seat in the back of the classroom. It was certainly better than the mean comments that she used to get, but she wasn't sure if she should be worried or not.

Mrs. Crisp came into the classroom and sat down at the desk in the front of the room preparing to do a role call for attendance. She looked down at a paper with her list of student names glancing up as she called out each name. When she came to Ann Dee she did a double take as she said Ann's name and glanced at Ann sitting at her desk. There was a pause and then Mrs. Crisp continued through the rest of the student list.

The first lesson of the morning was to review the multiplication tables. The class followed along with Mrs. Crisp as she wrote on the chalk board starting off with multiplication by ones, then twos, and on through to nines. The class followed along out loud as each problem was written on the board. Ann found the problems easy and liked when certain numbers like five and nine were used to multiply other numbers with. The results were interesting as patterns came out in the answers.

When they had gone through the multiplication exercise Mrs. Crisp introduced division to the class explaining how it was the opposite of multiplication. She had them work through several examples of dividing the answers to the multiplication they had been doing by numbers that had been multiplied together.

The answers worked out even when, say 30 was divided by the number 5 and 6 was the answer. Ann wondered what you did when the number 30 was divided by a number like 4. She knew that the answer wouldn't be even, but she didn't ask her question out loud. Ann didn't want to open herself up to the taunts of her classmates. She hoped that she could find the answer in one of the books on the bookshelf at home.

As she thought about this the recess bell went off and she and the other students put their classroom things away in their desks and she pulled out her bag of jacks so that she would have something to do during recess.

The rest of the girls went out on the grass and started to jump rope while the boys headed over to the baseball diamond and chased each other around.

Ann went over by the concrete walkway near the school building and spilled the jacks on the concrete. Then she squatted down and started bouncing the ball, scooping up first one jack, then two, then three, and so on. She was concentrating hard as she knew it was harder for her to fit much more than six or seven jacks in her hand as well as the ball.

"Hey, Ann, would you come over and help us with the jump ropes?" it was Kathi.

Ann could hardly believe what she heard.

"Me?"

"Yes, we need another person on the jump ropes so we can do 'Double Dutch'."

Ann picked up her jacks and put them into her little bag. She got up and she and Kathi went over to where the other girls were playing.

"What do I need to do?" asked Ann.

"It's easy. You take a jump rope in each hand and turn them in opposite directions. Just watch Betty. She will have the other end of the ropes and will sing a song so we get a rhythm."

"I've never done this."

"Don't worry, Ann, just follow what I do," said Betty, "and follow the song."

Betty took the ends of two of the jump ropes and Ann took hold of the opposite ends.

Betty said, "Okay, now start with me and keep in time with the song."

Ann tried her best to swing the ropes like Betty. First one went clockwise and the other went in the other direction. Ann's arms had to stretch to keep the ropes going.

"Relax, Ann, let the rhythm keep you in time," Kathi said.

Betty started the song:

Down in the valley

Where the green grass grows

Sat little Mary

As sweet as a rose

She sang so high, she sang so sweet

Along came Danny and kissed her on the cheek

How many kisses did she get?

1, 2, 3, 4, ...

Ann blushed and smiled, but kept up the rhythm as Mary jumped into the middle and skipped the double ropes in time with the song. Mary stayed jumping until they reached twenty and then jumped out. They repeated the song putting in Kathi's name and Kathi jumped in to the count of twelve and then she jumped out. Mary came over to take the ropes from Ann, still staying in time.

"Go ahead, Ann, you jump," said Mary.

"Yes, give it a try," said Kathi.

Ann got ready watching the ropes as they were swung around in great circles and listened to the song.

Down in the valley

Where the green grass grows

Sat little Annie

As sweet as a rose

She sang so high, she sang so sweet

Along came Danny and kissed her on the cheek

How many kisses did she get?

1, 2, 3, 4, ...

Ann jumped in as the count started and made it up to five before she jumped out. She was smiling and exhausted. They put her back on the rope so that Betty could have a turn and then the bell for the end of recess rang.

It was the first time that Ann had ever come in with the other girls of the class. She didn't say much, but the girls were all happy with how they had done.

The students sat down at their desks again and Mrs. Crisp reminded them that their summer break was less than two weeks off and that they would be given a reading list this summer. They were to read at least three of the books on the list over the summer and be prepared to write a report on one of them when they came back to the next grade. Mrs. Crisp passed out copies of the list to the students at the front of each row and had the students pass them to the rear so that Everyone would have a copy.

Mrs. Crisp then had them line up at the classroom door to go to the cafeteria for lunch. When they were all lined up she opened the door and they followed her to the lunchroom. They lined up to go through the food line to pick up their trays, napkins, and flatware before they moved on to get their lunch food.

Ann picked up her tray and then moved on through the line choosing food that would be easy for her to eat and ending up with a small carton of milk and a straw. She swung toward a table that she usually sat at when Kathi came up beside her.

"Come on over here with us, Ann."

They walked over to a table where Mary and Betty were sitting.

Ann sat down across from Kathi and put down her tray. This is something that she never imagined. She wasn't sitting alone at lunch. She was both excited and a bit apprehensive. The girls talked about what they did over the weekend and what clothes they were hoping to get now that summer was coming. Ann just ate and listened, being careful to eat her food a little at a time.

Mary asked Ann what she had done over the weekend. Ann carefully swallowed what she was chewing, took a sip of milk, and positioned her hand in front of her mouth while she explained how her father took her out to where a bridge was being worked on. Then when they went to a diner for lunch and finally saw a beautiful rainbow on the way home.

The other girls had been quiet while Ann recounted her adventures. Then Ann stopped talking. She was not sure if she had said something wrong or not.

"Ann, did you really get to see a bridge up close?" asked Kathi.

"Is that what your father does?" asked Mary.

"What does your mother do?" asked Betty.

Ann explained, that yes, her father was an engineer who worked on big things like bridges and that her mother had gone to school to be an engineer, but now taught music and played the piano.

"Can you play the piano?" asked Kathi.

"Yes, I'm just learning, but I can play some on the piano."

"Wow!"

There were more questions coming when the bell rang for them to line up and head back to the classroom. The girls whispered some more questions to Ann until Mrs. Crisp called for them to be quiet with no talking while they headed back to their room.

Chapter 14

That afternoon Mrs. Crisp had the students open their literature books and do some reading. She would pick a student to read a paragraph or two of the story they were working on. The other students would follow along while the paragraphs were read aloud.

This story was about the moon. It talked about how the moon goes around the earth in an orbit and why it is sometimes a full moon and other times only part of it is lit up. It explained how the sun causes it to shine even at night.

Ann found the reading easy, but was glad that she was not called upon to read out loud. She also found the facts about the moon interesting.

When they had finished the story about the moon, Mrs. Crisp decided to read them some chapters out of a book, *Charlotte's Web*, by E. B. White. It was an interesting story about a pig named Wilbur, a spider named Charlotte, and a little girl named Fern.

Ann enjoyed listening to her teacher's voice and thinking about the characters in the story. She wondered how it would be to live out in the country where she could be on a farm with animals. She closed her eyes and put her head down on her desk and continued to listen as the story unfolded as she imagined what it must have been like on the farm.

The next thing she knew the final bell rang and it was time for the students to clear their desks and line up to go to the buses. Ann remembered to bring the summer reading list with her as well as her bag of jacks. She didn't need to bring any books home with her tonight.

Kathi, Mary, and Betty took another bus home so Ann sat alone in her usual seat. She was happy though as she thought about how different recess and lunch were that day.

The minutes passed and there was the familiar squeal of the school bus brakes and Ann was getting off at her house with Buster eagerly awaiting her arrival.

Ann walked to the steps and then bent down to give Buster a hug as his tail whipped around sweeping the air and brushing off the front steps. She opened the front door and walked into the front room where her mother was playing the piano.

"Hello, Princess!"

"Hi, Mom."

"How was your day at school today?"

"It was wonderful, Mom. Mrs. Crisp gave us a reading list for the summer and I jumped rope with the other girls at recess."

"Oh my but that must have been fun. What books do they want you to read this summer?"

"I brought a paper home with the list. I don't remember them all. We are supposed to read at least three books from the list and then write a report on one of them."

"Why don't you put the list up on the corkboard in the kitchen? Then we can check off what books you read as the summer progresses."

Ann went into the kitchen and used thumbtacks to attach the list to the corkboard.

"Mom, do we have a book called *Charlotte's Web*?"

"I don't think so, Princess. Is it on your summer reading list?"

"No, the teacher was reading it to us this afternoon and I wondered if we had it so I could read it at home. I loved listening to the story and I wonder what it would be like to live on a farm."

"Maybe one weekend we can go out into the country and visit a farm."

"That would be so much fun, Mom."

"How would you like to practice the piano for a while?"

"Okay, Mom."

Her mother gave Ann some keyboard exercises to warm up with and then had her play a couple of the pieces of music they had learned over the weekend. Ann was improving and getting much smoother with her fingers on the keyboard. They even played the keyboard at the same time. Her mother showed her how to read the music and play the higher scales while her mother played the tempo. Ann thought it was wonderful that even though they played different notes the music sounded beautiful. They spent a good part of the afternoon playing together until her mother had to work on getting their supper ready.

"You go ahead and play by yourself, Princess, while I work on supper."

Ann practiced while her mother went into the kitchen. The piano didn't sound as nice as it did when they were playing together, but Ann felt that she was getting a bit better. She played a piece of music that her mother had introduced to her over the weekend and found that it was now a lot easier, even though she made a mistake or two. Finally Ann decided that she was too tired and gave up for the time being. She went into the kitchen to watch her mother.

"Is Dad going to be late getting home today?"

"I don't think so. He hasn't called to tell me that he is going to be late."

"What are we having for dinner tonight?"

"What would you like, Princess?"

Ann thought about that. She wondered if they had any chicken. She couldn't think of a vegetable that she wanted, though.

"Can we have chicken?"

"Sure, I have plenty of time to bake a chicken for us. What would you like with that? Is there a vegetable that you haven't had for a while?"

"I am not sure about a vegetable, Mom. Could we have your biscuits?"

"That's a great idea. How about a salad with that? I have some carrots and radishes we can add to some lettuce."

"Perfect, Mom."

Ann watched as her mother got things ready for baking. The chicken took almost no time at all to prepare. Then her mother took out a large bowl and added flour, butter, baking powder, a beaten egg, some sugar, and milk to make the dough for the biscuits. Then she took out a square baking pan and greased it with butter before putting in the dough. The oven was hot and ready for the chicken. She looked at the clock and decided to wait ten or fifteen minutes before putting it in.

She pulled some lettuce out of the refrigerator along with the carrots and radishes. After giving them a good rinse in the sink she got out the cutting board and chopped the carrots and radishes into bite sized pieces. Then it was time to put in the chicken.

"That will take about an hour and in half that time we can put in the biscuits. Your father should be home just about when it is all done."

"What do we do now, Mom?"

"Why don't we take a look at that summer reading list that you brought home?" Ann's mother went over to the corkboard and removed the list so they could both look at it at the kitchen table.

There were nine books listed. Ann and her mother read through each of the titles.

Brighty of the Grand Canyon

Wind in the Willows

Hurry Home, Candy

Mystery of Holly Lane

The Silver Chair

Otis Spofford

The Queen Elizabeth Story

The Borrowers

and

Moccasin Trail

"These titles look interesting. We will have to get over to the library and see if we can find out more about each of the stories," said her mother.

"When can we do that, Mom?"

"This Saturday, I should think."

"Do we have any of these books at home?"

"I think we might have *Wind in the Willows,* shall we take a look?"

"Sure!"

Ann and her mother went to the staircase and climbed to where the book shelves were. Ann took an extra step so that she could search the titles above the shelves that she usually looked. Her mother could see the uppermost shelves.

"Here it is, Ann."

Ann's mother reached for a book up on the top shelf and pulled it down.

"Oh, Mom, can we read it?"

"Not right now, Princess. I've got to keep an eye on supper, but you can take it in the front room and look through it on the couch there."

Ann took the heavy book to the couch and opened it up. Buster came over and did his best to snuggle with her on the couch. She first flipped through the pages and looked at the illustrations. There were many different animals that were the characters in the book. They were dressed up in clothes and even drove an old fashioned car. She flipped back to the beginning and started to read the story herself.

Chapter 15

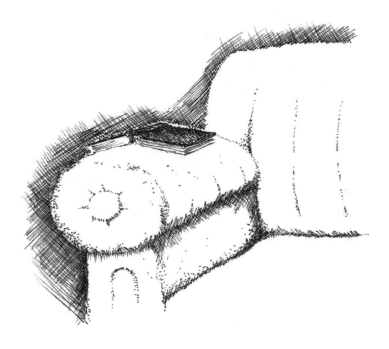

Over a half an hour had gone by and Ann's mother checked on the chicken in the oven. It was coming along quite nicely. It was time to put the biscuits in the oven.

Just then the front door opened and Andy entered the front room.

"Hello, everybody, I'm home!"

"Hi, Daddy, I'm reading a book called *Wind in the Willows*."

"That's a wonderful book. You will enjoy it. Let me talk to your mother. I'll be back in a Moment."

Her father went into the kitchen and she could hear her parents talking. Her mother was surprised that he was home a bit early. Her father told her that he was being asked to manage a new project, but he needed to talk to her about it because it would mean some changes.

Ann was interested in hearing, but she was also interested in the book. She went back to where a mole and a water rat were about to row along the river. She was so engrossed in the story that she was surprised to hear her mother call her to supper. She put the book on the arm of the couch so she wouldn't lose the page and slipped off the couch on to the floor.

"I just need to wash my hands," she answered back and skipped into the bathroom to clean up. When she got to the kitchen table her father was putting some dressing on each of their salads before bringing them to the table.

"Go ahead and sit down, Princess. I will have the chicken and biscuits on your plates in just a Moment."

Ann found her place at the table and sat down, putting her napkin in her lap. Her father helped her mother serve the plates and then they both sat down.

The chicken and biscuits smelled wonderful. Ann picked up a biscuit and bit off a piece feeling it almost melt in her mouth. Then she picked up her fork and started on the salad. Her mother had thoughtfully made sure that the lettuce pieces were extra small for her so it would be easy for her to eat. Next she ate some of the chicken. It was tender and moist with a touch of rosemary flavor.

"Your father has some news he'd like to share," said Ann's mother.

Ann looked up at her father and he began to speak.

"I have been asked to manage a new project for the firm. Only this project is not near here. It is in a town in another state and I will have to fly out of town to the construction location for a couple of days. I need to fly out tomorrow and I won't return home until Thursday. It's an important project so I am excited to be asked to manage it, but I feel bad about leaving you two for so long."

"We'll be okay, Daddy. You won't be gone that long. I just wish that I could fly in a plane, too."

"I'll get a ride to the airport tomorrow morning so I can leave the car here for your mother to use."

"Are you working on another bridge, Daddy?"

"Not this time. It will be a big project that will involve the construction of a dam for flood control as well as hydroelectric power."

"What kind of power?"

"Hydroelectric is when you use water to spin a generator that makes electricity."

"Will I be able to see it like I did the bridge project?"

Andy looked at Ann's mother. "I'm not sure, Princess; it is a long way away. It is not like a Saturday adventure like we did last weekend."

"After you have finished your supper, Ann, I'll need your help doing the dishes. Your father needs to pack for his trip."

"Okay, Mom."

Ann enjoyed the meal and helped her mother clear the table and clean the dishes while her father got prepared for his trip. After they were done, Ann's mother went upstairs to see if she could help Andy.

Ann went into the front room and took the *Wind in the Willows* book off the arm of the couch and headed out in the back yard so she could sit under the large tree with the big roots. Buster followed and lay beside her with his snout on her knee.

Chapter 16

Ann felt a hand on her shoulder shaking her awake. It was her father and it was dark enough out to be twilight time.

"Time to head inside, Princess."

She stretched and looked at what page she was on in the book. She backed up a couple of pages and memorized that page number. It was sixteen. She brought the book inside with her and placed it on the small table in the front room.

"Daddy, what time will you be flying in an airplane?"

"It is supposed to take off about nine in the morning. I will have to get there a bit earlier though, so I'll have my friend Billy pick me up before your school bus comes. That will give him time to drive me to the airport well before the plane takes off."

"So I'll see you at breakfast, then?"

"For sure, Princess."

"Good. I'm going to go upstairs to bed. Goodnight, Dad."

"Goodnight, Princess."

Ann climbed the stairs and headed to her bedroom. Her mother was in the bathroom getting ready for bed.

"Hi, Mom, I'm going to sleep. See you in the morning."

"Goodnight, Princess. You and I will have a good time while your father is gone on his trip. Sweet dreams."

Ann hung up her school clothes and got in her bed. Duster was still sitting in the window watching the world go by and taking naps. Buster came in and made sure that Ann was okay then he went back downstairs to check on the rest of the house before he finally returned and curled up in his bedtime box.

In the morning everyone was up for breakfast in plenty of time. Ann was excited for her father and still a little jealous that he would get to fly in an airplane. After breakfast Ann went upstairs and brushed her teeth. Then she went and got in her school clothes. Her mother called her into the bathroom so she could help her get her hair ready.

"My, don't you look nice today."

It was her father as he walked by the bathroom with his luggage. He was dressed in a shirt and tie and wore a sports jacket.

"You look nice too, Daddy."

"Thanks you, Princess."

Ann's mother was done with Ann's hair and let her head downstairs.

Ann decided that she would leave her jacks at home today and see what might happen at recess.

"I think that is Billy's car I hear," said her father to her mother.

Her mother gave Andy a big hug and a kiss. Ann wasn't certain, but it looked like her mother was about to cry.

"I'll give you a phone call after I get on the ground Dear. I love you both." Andy gave Ann a squeeze and patted her on the head.

Andy grabbed his suitcase and headed out the door and crossed the front yard to Billy's car. He threw his bag in the back seat and then got into the front seat, waving goodbye. Ann waived goodbye and felt her mother behind her clutching her by the shoulders. As Billy and her father drove off, Ann's mother grabbed her apron and dabbed at her eyes.

In just a few minutes the school bus arrived with its brakes squealing. Usually Ann waited for the bus alone, but this morning her mother had stood with her.

"Goodbye, Ann. Have a good day at school."

"'Bye, Mom!"

Ann climbed onto the school bus and went back to her seat wondering what her day would be like today.

Chapter 17

The day went by fast for Ann. Mrs. Crisp had more reviews of multiplication to have the class work on. She passed out a sheet of paper to each of them with multiplication problems on it. They put their names on the paper and then filled in the answers. The papers were collected and it was time for recess.

Mary and Kathi made sure that Ann went with them and they met Betty where Ann usually played with jacks, only this time Betty had taken some chalk and drawn out some boxes on the concrete surface. They had numbers in the boxes and Ann knew they were going to play hopscotch. They had a lot of fun and Ann was tired by the time recess ended.

After lunch Mrs. Crisp passed back the papers they had worked on prior to recess. Ann had an "A" written on her paper and a note from Mrs. Crisp telling her that she did a perfect job.

Later in the afternoon their teacher read more of the story *Charlotte's Web*. Ann listened with great interest. She wondered again what it would be like to live on a real farm in the country.

Soon it was time for school to end and Ann had to get to her bus. She said goodbye to Mary, Kathi, and Betty, heading for her own bus.

When it arrived at her stop not only was Buster waiting for her, but her mother as well.

"Hi, Mom!"

"Hello, Princess. I hope you had a good day at school."

"It was a good day. The teacher read some more of *Charlotte's Web* to us and we did some multiplication problems. Here is my paper. I got all of them right!"

"That's wonderful! We need to put this on the corkboard so that your father can see it when he gets back home." Her mother took the paper and went into the kitchen and mounted it on the corkboard for all to see.

"I think this deserves something special. Why don't you and I take a drive downtown and visit the Parnassus book store. We can take your summer book list and see if we can't find out about some of the titles. What do you think about that?"

"Oh, could we? That would be fun."

"Let me get some money out of the cookie jar and you get your reading list off the corkboard."

Ann's mother went into the kitchen and reached up high to a shelf next to the kitchen sink where a crockery cookie jar sat and brought it down to the counter. She took off the lid and reached inside pulling out a few dollar bills. Then she put the top back on and placed the jar back on the shelf.

"That should be enough. Are you ready, Ann?"

"Yes, Mom."

Her mother grabbed the car key off one of the hooks on the kitchen wall and they headed for the front door. Once outside her mother locked the front door and they went to the car.

"Mom, may I sit in the front seat?"

"I think so, but I will need your help moving the booster seat to the front."

Ann's mother struggled to unhitch the booster seat until it finally came loose. Then she put in the front passenger side of the bench seat and worked to attach it firmly enough that Ann could get in it and fasten a seat belt around herself.

A Moment later they were off. Her mother piloted the car around the streets crossing several blocks before she turned left onto a long street. Soon, after a few traffic lights, they pulled into a small parking lot and found a spot to park. It was a short walk from there to the book store. They entered through a side door and immediately the smell of old books surrounded them. The shelves went from floor to ceiling and some light came from above. It was a mix of sunlight and electrical light as there were skylights letting in light through the roof of the building.

There were small signs on the shelves indicating the types of books that would be found there. Some were historical and others were mystery book. Some were engineering and some were fantasy. As they explored the different shelves of books a little lady approached them. She had light grey hair done up in a bun on her head and her dress was covered with a pattern of flowers. She wore black framed half glasses that were perched near the end of her nose and she held three books clasped tightly to her chest.

"May I help you?" she asked.

"Yes," answered Ann's mother, "we have a list of books for summer reading and we would like to see if you have any of them." She handed the list to the woman who put her pile of books down on a nearby shelf and slid her glasses up on her nose so she could read the list.

"Hmm, I believe that we have most of these. Would you follow me, please, and we can take a look in the children's section."

They followed the lady toward the back and then she took a right turn to another wing of the store. This one was even brighter and had some newer books.

"Did you want all of these books?"

"No, we already have a couple of them at home and a few of them we wanted to see if they were interesting or not."

"What ones do you have already?"

"*The Wind in the Willows* and *The Borrowers*."

"Very good, we can eliminate those. Here are a couple of books from the list. They are mystery adventure books."

The lady pulled down copies of *Mystery of Holly Lane* and *The Silver Chair*.

"What is your name young lady?"

"Ann."

"My name is Miss Fernwood. I will help you decide which of these books are right for you, but first a question. Are you reading any of these books now?"

"Yes, I've started *The Wind in the Willows*."

"And how do you like it?"

"It is wonderful."

"How difficult do you find it to read, Ann?"

"I like it. I understand the words and enjoy the story. I haven't had to ask my Mom or Dad for help yet"

"That sounds good, Ann. I think a couple of the books on your list might be too young for you then. It says that you need to read three of these on the list. Let me suggest that you look at; *Otis Spofford, The Mystery of Holly Lane,* and *Hurry Home Candy*."

She handed her the copy of *The Mystery of Holly Lane*.

"Take a look at this one while I go find the other two titles." Miss Fernwood went off to the other parts of the book shelves and gathered up two more books before she returned to Ann.

"Have you had a good look at *The Mystery of Holly Lane*?"

"Yes, I think it will be fun to read," replied Ann.

"Here are the other two I would recommend. Look them over and you and your mother can decide which ones you would like to purchase."

With that Miss Fernwood went off to other parts of the book shop. Ann and her mother looked over the books.

"What do think of these books, Ann?"

"Oh, Mom, I like them all."

"We have two of the books on the list at home. Why don't you pick one of these three to buy and bring back home with us?"

Ann struggled with trying to choose from the three books. She went from one to the other several times.

"How do I decide?"

"That's up to you, Princess. We can only afford one right now."

"Okay, I'd like *Hurry Home Candy*."

"I'm sure that's a good choice. Let's take it up to the register and pay for it."

They walked to the front of the store and found Miss Fernwood at the cash register, sorting through a pile of books.

"Well, I see that you made your choice. Oh my, that is a very good choice. I expect that you will enjoy it."

Ann's mother paid for the book and left the other two for Miss Fernwood to return to the proper shelf.

"Say thank you to Miss Fernwood, Ann."

"Thank you Miss Fernwood for helping me so much."

"You are very welcome young lady, please come and see us again."

Ann and her mother took the book and went out the front of the store. They turned to their right to get back to the parking lot. The sky was getting dark and the temperature was dropping. The gentle breeze was now turning into more of a wind. They hurried back to the car and got inside.

"Let's get back home, Ann. It looks like it's going to storm soon."

The ride back was windy and the sky got even darker. By the time they were parked in their driveway it was just starting to rain. They rushed to get inside their house and out of the wind.

"Whew, that was close. We made it."

Just then there was a bright flash from outside. A few seconds later there was the low rumble of thunder. That was followed by the sound of rain hammering down.

"Oh my, I need to close the windows! Ann, you go check upstairs and make sure that the windows are closed up there."

"Okay, Mom!"

Ann ran up the stairs as fast as she could. She went into her room and saw that Duster had already jumped from the window sill to escape the rain coming in through the window. Ann closed it and then checked her parent's room's windows. They also needed to be closed. Buster followed her as she dashed around the upstairs checking windows. When everything was checked and the open windows were closed Ann returned to the downstairs.

"All set, Mom."

"Thank you, Princess. My, what a storm we are having! Let me work on our supper. You can either help me or read or practice the piano."

"I'll help."

Chapter 18

So Ann and her mother fixed a delicious dinner for themselves just before the storm knocked out the power. Ann's mother brought out some candles and they ate by candlelight, which Ann thought was wonderful. Then they cleaned up the dishes and put everything away.

"What do we do now, Mom?"

The power flickered back on. They blew out the candles and went into the front room where her mother sat down at the piano and played some of the song she had been writing. Ann sat on the couch and closed her eyes listening to the words of the lyrics imagining how it would be to live by the sea.

"Did you ever live on the ocean, Mom?"

"My parents would take us to the beach in the summer, when I was young."

"Your song makes it seem so nice."

"It was, Ann. I hope we can live close enough to the ocean someday so we can go to the beach in the summer."

"Me, too."

The storm had calmed down for a while, but had come back with a fury now. The winds seemed to shake the house and rattle the windows. Duster and Buster were in the front room. Buster was on the couch with Ann and Duster was on the piano top curled up. Ann's mother stopped playing and listened to the wind howling.

"Why don't we get ready for bed? You can meet me in my bedroom and I'll read you a story."

"Which story, Mom?"

"We didn't finish *Treasure island* the other night. I can read that one."

"Okay!"

Ann gave Buster a pat and then got down from the couch. She went upstairs and into the bathroom to brush her teeth. Buster followed her up the stairs and Duster raised her head wondering where everyone was going.

Ann's mother went around to the kitchen to make sure that all the windows were closed shut and that the doors were locked for the night. Then she headed upstairs to get ready for bed herself. She stopped at the bookcase on the stairs to pick out their book for the night. Ann was coming out of the bathroom and heading for her room.

"Guess what, Mom?"

"What's that, Princess?"

"I was brushing my teeth and I felt with my tongue where my teeth came out and I can feel new ones coming in!"

"Let me see."

Ann bent her head back and opened her mouth wide so her mother could take a look.

"My goodness, the new ones are coming in! How wonderful. In a week or two they will fill the gap."

"I can hardly wait!"

Ann was so happy to think of her new teeth coming in and knowing that the big gap would soon be gone. She put her clothes on hangers and got into her pajamas.

"Buster, isn't it wonderful?"

Buster looked up at Ann and swished his tail back and forth his whole body swaying with the tail. Ann headed for her parent's bedroom and found her mother had turned down the covers and fluffed up the pillows.

"Let's curl up and I'll read you the story."

Ann jumped up onto the bed which was considerably higher off the floor than her own. Then she situated herself against the pillows while her mother turned on a reading light that was hooked over the back of the headboard and then went and turned off the main bedroom light.

"Are you ready, Ann?"

"Yes, Mom."

As the lightning and thunder continued, Ann's mother read the story to her. Buster curled up at the foot of the bed and listened, too. Duster was able to jump on the bed and found a comfortable spot to curl up at the foot of the bed. As she listened to the story about the young boy and his voyage to find a treasure on an island Ann rested her head against her mother's shoulder and visualized what it must have been like to live in the days of sailing ships and pirates.

Chapter 19

It was still raining when Ann woke up the next morning.

"Do I have to go to school, Mom?"

"Of course, Princess, the rain should stop by lunch time. And I have some piano lessons to give today. I need to be in another part of the city later this morning to give them. So come down for breakfast."

Ann sighed and came down for breakfast with her mother. It was a nice one of French toast and strawberries. When they were done Ann went upstairs to get cleaned up and dressed for school. Her mother did the dishes and put out food in the bowls on the kitchen floor for Buster and Duster. Then she went upstairs to help Ann with brushing her hair. The wet weather made Ann's hair even frizzier than usual, but her mother managed to get it to look neat and pretty, tying it up with a ribbon.

"Oh, Mom, what will I do? If I wear a rain hat, it will mess up my hair."

"I think we have a small umbrella that you can use today, Princess. That way you can wear a raincoat but not a rain hat. Just be sure not to forget to bring the umbrella home with you this afternoon."

They got themselves all ready for their day and got downstairs to the front door just before the school bus arrived. Ann held the umbrella over herself and got to the bus only to find that she didn't know how to collapse the umbrella so that she could get in the bus's door. Her mother rushed over and showed her the catch that released the mechanism so it would fold up. Then she gave Ann a quick kiss on the cheek and off the bus went.

Ann's day at school was a good one with more math problems and reading in the afternoon. They didn't have morning recess outside because of the rain so they were allowed to get into small groups and play with each other for that time period. Afternoon recess was also inside since it was so muddy outside. Mrs. Crisp read them another couple of chapters from *Charlotte's Web*.

Ann was heading for the bus when she realized that she had forgotten the umbrella so she raced back to the classroom to retrieve it. Mrs. Crisp was standing at the door with the umbrella and a little smile on her face as she handed it to Ann.

"Thank you, Mrs. Crisp."

"You're welcome, Ann. Have a good evening."

Ann ran back to the bus port and Mrs. Crisp called to her.

"Don't run, Ann, you will still make your bus and you don't want to slip and fall."

Ann slowed down. She did make it to her bus with plenty of time and found her seat. The ride home was uneventful with the familiar squeal of the bus's brakes as it stopped by her house. She jumped off and walked up to the front steps. The afternoon sun had dried up most of the puddles and the grass and plants seemed to have grown another inch or two since the morning.

Her mother was at the front door to greet her.

"How was your day?"

"Fine, Mom, how did the lessons go?"

"My student is getting better. He is making progress, but it is slow."

Her mother helped her off with her raincoat and took the umbrella and placed it in the umbrella stand.

"Have you heard from Daddy?"

"Yes, I did. He called this morning to say that he will be back tomorrow afternoon."

"Oh, boy!"

"Yes, I'll be glad to have him back home, too. Why don't you get out of your school clothes and into some comfortable things? We can spend some time on your piano lessons this afternoon."

Ann went upstairs and changed. The window to her room was open and the sunshine came in along with a slight breeze. The weather had gotten warm since the rain in the morning. Duster was in the window enjoying the warm sun and watching the birds fly around the yard.

Ann and her mother spent time playing the piano until it was time to get supper prepared. Ann was making progress and spent more time playing while her mother worked on their dinner. After dinner they went for a walk while it was still light out. As they got home the phone rang. It was Andy. He talked with Ann's mother for a few minutes and then Ann was allowed to talk to him a little.

"Hi, Daddy, Mom says that you are coming home tomorrow."

"Yes, Princess, it will be late in the afternoon when my plane gets in. I am looking forward to being home again. I miss the two of you."

"I miss you, too, Daddy."

"Alright, Princess, let me talk to your Mom. I'll see you tomorrow."

Ann handed the phone back to her mother and went into the front room to find the *Wind in the Willows* book. She found it on the small table next to the couch and tried to remember the page number that would get her back to where she had been in the book. She thought hard. Sixteen! That was the number. She turned to page sixteen with a smile and found where she had left off.

Chapter 20

By the afternoon of the next day Ann was home from school and excited with the thought of her father coming back home.

"When will he get here, Mom?"

"I am hoping around supper time. What would you like to do until it's time to make dinner?""

"Would you teach me the music you wrote on the piano?"

"Sure, we can practice some of it. It is probably a little more difficult than some of the other music you've learned, but let's try it."

Ann and her mother worked on the music for quite a while with her mother showing her the different parts and letting her try to learn the tune. Ann was getting smoother and wanted to try to sing the words, too. Her mother sang the lyrics until Ann was comfortable playing the music enough so that she could join in singing.

The time went by and eventually Ann's mother had to start on fixing the dinner.

"Why don't you keep playing, Ann, and I'll work on supper. You are really coming along well."

Ann smiled and went back to playing the piano and doing her best to sing along with the music. In a few minutes wonderful smells came from the kitchen and Ann stopped her playing, got down from the piano bench and went into the kitchen to see what her mother was preparing.

"What are you making, Mom, it smells delicious?"

"Chicken pot pie."

"Will Daddy be here soon?"

"I hope so. His plane should have landed and he is getting a ride home with one of the men he works with."

Just then the front door opened.

"Hello beautiful ladies!"

"It's Daddy!"

Ann and her mother rushed into Andy's open arms as he dropped his luggage. They hugged each other as they laughed and cried. At least Ann's mother cried. She was so happy to have Andy back home.

"Hey, I have a couple of presents for you both."

Andy reached into his coat pocket and pulled out a bottle.

"It's real maple syrup. We can have it when your mother makes pancakes or waffles."

Ann looked at the bottle of amber liquid. It moved about slowly when she turned the bottle upside down. The label was in the shape of a tree leaf, a maple leaf.

"This is for you, my Sweet."

Out of another pocket he pulled out a tin box. It also had a maple leaf on it.

"It is a box of maple sugar candy. It is some very sweet stuff."

"Oh my, Andy, I haven't had any real maple sugar candy for such a long time!" exclaimed Ann's mother.

"Where have you been, Daddy?"

"I've been in northern New England."

"Is that across the ocean, Daddy?"

"No, Ann, it's in the north east part of the country. They call it New England because it was where some of the first people from England came over to start what became the United States. It consists of six states: Vermont, New Hampshire, Maine, Massachusetts, Connecticut, and Rhode Island. I was in Vermont working on a project there. It is a part of the country that they make maple syrup, so I brought back some with me."

"Well, dinner is ready to come out of the oven so why don't you both get ready to eat. I need to make sure things don't burn."

"We can't have that. Alright, Princess, you go wash your hands and I will put my bags away. I'll be down in just a minute."

Ann got ready for dinner and then helped her mother get the salads ready. Andy came back downstairs in time for the plates with the chicken pot pie to be served.

"Mmmm, dinner smells delicious and it is so nice to be back home."

"What was it like flying, Daddy?"

"It was okay, but it was noisy and I spent most of my time doing work."

"What did you think of the project?" asked Ann's mother.

"I'm glad that I was able to get involved while it was still in the beginning stages. They have a lot of things that need to be considered in order to make it successful. I like the project, but it will be a long one."

"How long will it take?"

"At least two years, I think. That brings up something we need to talk about. If I am going to take this project it *will* mean that we'll need to move to Vermont."

Ann's mother looked over at Ann. "What do you think about that, Princess?"

Ann thought about it. She had no idea where Vermont was and what it was like. "I don't know. Would I get to fly in an airplane?"

"You might, though it's more likely that we would drive our car so we can have it where we move to."

"Do you like it in Vermont?"

"I found it a very nice place. It is not like the city here. It is more like the country with lots of trees and hills."

"Is it near the ocean?"

"No, but nearby there is a large lake."

"What do you think, Mommy?"

"I think that it will mean a lot of change, but I also think Vermont would be a lovely place for us to live."

Ann thought about the prospect of moving. She would go to a new school and miss the friends that she had just made. There would be a different house to live in, but Buster and Duster would move with them. She would get to live in the country and might even be close to a farm like the one in *Charlotte's Web*. She wondered if there were any books on Vermont in their library.

"Since everyone did such a good job with cleaning their dinner plates, why don't we each have some of that maple sugar candy that I brought back from Vermont?"

Andy opened the metal box with the maple leaf on the top and handed Ann and her mother a piece of candy shaped like a maple leaf. It was thick and a light amber color with a look as if it were cast from brown sugar.

Ann tasted her piece and found it was not only sweet, but had an especially nice flavor.

"I *love* this, Daddy!"

"It's made from the sap of a special maple tree. It is collected from the trees in metal pails and then boiled in a large vat. It becomes the maple syrup that we will have with our pancakes this weekend and it is heated some more to form the crystal sugar that the candy is made from."

"When will we move to Vermont?"

"It will probably take a couple of weeks to find a place to live there and then we will need to pack up all our things into a moving van and drive to Vermont."

"Do we have any books on Vermont, Daddy?"

"We can look in our collection, and then there is always the library."

"I need some help with the dishes. Who wants to volunteer?"

"I will, Mom."

"While you girls work on that I'll bring my bags upstairs and unpack. I'll also see if we have any books on Vermont."

Andy went off to get those things done while Ann and her mother cleaned up the supper dishes.

"How do you feel about moving, Ann?"

"I think it will be okay, how about you, Mom?"

"I grew up in New England, so for me it will be like going back home."

"Really?"

"Yes, it has been many years since I lived there. The college I went to was here in the Midwest and after I met your father he found his first job here. So we stayed here, got married, and then you arrived."

By that time they had cleaned up everything in the kitchen. It was getting late and Ann's father found a book on New England with a chapter on Vermont.

Ann brought the book up to her room and got ready for bed. She thought more about what it would be like to move to a new place. As she brushed her teeth she was reminded of how her new teeth were coming in. She needed to let her father know and she wanted to tell her friends in school of how she would be moving. Maybe she could get their addresses and they could write each other. She wondered how they would move Duster and Buster to the new place. She also wondered what their new house would be like. She opened the book to the section on

Vermont and looked at the pictures first. Then she started reading. This next part of her life was going to be exciting.

It wasn't long before Ann fell asleep dreaming about maple trees covered with candy leaves. She grabbed one off a branch and ran out of the forest and on through a grassy field toward a red barn. There was a talking pig there telling her to be careful of the spider webs. A cow asked her if she would like to climb into the hay loft and bring her down some hay. She climbed a wooden ladder. A voice called to her from somewhere far away. It was a boy her age standing below in the barn. He waved to her and said, "Hi, my name is Bennett."

Made in the USA
Middletown, DE
12 March 2019